Antediluvian Tales

Antediluvian Tales

Poppy Z. Brite

SUBTERRANEAN PRESS 2007

First Edition

ISBN:
978-1-59606-116-3

Subterranean Press
PO Box 190106
Burton, MI 48519

www.subterraneanpress.com

Table of Contents

This one's for Chris.

I come to you and you see me whole ... You love me all the way around the equator and not just for some story I wrote. When your door closes and the world's outside, we're eye to eye.

—Stephen King, *Lisey's Story*

Drink Up, Dreamers, You're Running Dry:

A Foreword to *Antediluvian Tales*

F irst off, this little book and its title are self-explanatory and, I hope, user-friendly. If you're the sort of person who usually skips forewords and introductions, please don't feel obliged to read this one unless you'd like a bit of elucidation about the concept and a couple of suggestions on various ways in which the book may be read.

The title of this foreword is from Peter Gabriel's 1977 song "Here Comes the Flood." Seventeen months (at this writing) after the post-Katrina failure of the federal levees, I still can't listen to this song with dry eyes. Gabriel has said that he wrote the lyrics after having a dream in which people's thoughts became visible: "I was referring to a mental flood ... a release, a wash over the mind."[1] Even so, as song lyrics do with unnerving frequency, the lines seemed to do an uncannily accurate job of describing events that would take place more than a quarter-century after the song was recorded.

The title of this collection, *Antediluvian Tales*, is both a reference to Gabriel's song and to the fact that I feel my own work has been irrevocably split into two periods: Pre-K and Post-K. I usually wait until I have enough stories for a full-length book—twelve or thirteen at least—before beginning to collect them. After the events of 2005, though, I couldn't see pairing stories I'd written before the flood with

---

[1] http://www.songfacts.com

those I'd written after; for better or worse, my life, my outlook, and, necessarily, my work has changed forever. Except for the final piece in the book—"The Last Good Day of My Life," a nonfiction look at the changes the past two years have wrought on me, filtered through a reminiscence about a day I spent knocking around Cairns, Australia not long before the storm—these are literally antediluvian tales, stories written before August 29, 2005. I've written plenty of work since then, and I hope it is good work, but I could no more pair any of it with these stories than I could raise a family of kittens in the basement of my flooded, ruined house. Whatever else they may be, the stories in this little collection now seem almost impossibly innocent to me.

Most of the stories herein have to do with the Stubbs family, the New Orleans clan whose adventures I have also chronicled in my Liquor novels, my novella D*U*C*K, and a few of the short stories in my previous collection, The Devil You Know. I've arranged the stories in the order that seems most aesthetically pleasing to me. If you'd prefer to read them in chronological order (the chronology of the characters' lives, that is, not the order in which I wrote them; for the latter information, please see the copyrights page), I've included an appendix that provides a chronology for the Stubbs family stories in Antediluvian Tales and—for completeness' sake—The Devil You Know. I owe a debt of thanks for this idea to Caitlín R. Kiernan, who included such an appendix in her short story collection Tales of Pain and Wonder (Gauntlet Press, 2000) to intriguing effect.

The remaining two pieces of fiction in this book, "Crown of Thorns" and "Wound Man and Horned Melon Go to Hell," are not Stubbs family stories. They are a matched set of their own, though: likely the last two tales I'll write about my fictitious, fluidly gendered alter ego, Dr. Brite, the coroner of New Orleans. I agonized over how to arrange these two stories, as reading them in one order leaves quite a different taste in your mouth than the other. Since I see Dr. Brite as a melancholy, somewhat self-defeating character probably not destined for long-term happiness, I've arranged them in the order that leaves less room for hope about Dr. Brite's relationship with Hank. If you want to be optimistic, by all means read "Wound Man and Horned Melon Go to Hell" *before* "Crown of Thorns." I've no objection to people projecting a little surplus optimism onto me or my alter ego; we could probably use it.

Before August 29, 2005, "antediluvian" was simply a word to me, a pretty Biblical reference that had a nice ring to it but no real personal resonance for me. I vaguely understood that it connoted a state of innocence, but I couldn't have imagined how deeply I would long for that innocence one day. Right now, everything I write is postdiluvian. Someday I hope to move on to *non*-diluvian work, to somehow get beyond all this and concern myself with other things. I think that day will be long in coming, though, and the only way I know of processing things is by writing about them. For now, I'll treasure my antediluvian tales for the things they do not know lie ahead of them, for the relative happiness and mental health of the person who wrote them, and for the city that exists in them, the city that will never exist in that form again, the city where we're currently trying to build a new life.

And if we break before the dawn, they'll use up what we used to be.

—Peter Gabriel, "Here Comes the Flood"

—Poppy Z. Brite
New Orleans, LA, January 2007

The Feast of St. Rosalie

"Rosalie, babe, you seen the tinferl?" said Alice Cannizzaro. "I hope I ain't left it by the meatball cone tent. I don't feel like walking all the way back over there." Alice had tripped over one of her grandchildren on the stairs a few weeks ago and currently wore a boot cast on her left foot.

"I'll go over and check," said Rosalie Stubbs. "No, hang on, here it is." She picked up the box of foil and handed it to Alice, who tore off a long piece and covered a steaming pan of lasagna. Rosalie took a red scrunchie from her purse and pulled her heavy black hair into a tail at the back of her neck. Alice was wearing a hair net, but Rosalie couldn't stand that.

They were setting up the Our Lady of Perpetual Help Altar Society's food tent at the Italian-American Heritage Festival in Kenner, about fifteen miles up the river from New Orleans. As well as the lasagna, they had two dozen stuffed artichokes Rosalie had made, and her little brother was supposed to be on the way with a pan of eggplant Parmesan. It still seemed strange to be living way out here. Rosalie had been born and raised in New Orleans' Lower Ninth Ward, an inner-city working class neighborhood sandwiched

between the Industrial Canal and the parish line. To her, Kenner
felt like the sleepy little town it had been a hundred and two years
ago when her namesake, St. Rosalie, saved its livestock from the
anthrax. The immigrant farmers remembered the saint from Sicily
and prayed until she came through for them as she had done during Palermo's plague epidemic in 1624. Tomorrow was her feast
day, when Our Lady's parishioners would deck the statue in ribbons and parade her through the streets of Kenner in commemo-
ration as they did every year.

After her divorce, Rosalie had reverted to her maiden name,
taken her two children, and moved back in with her parents. When
that got old, she found a place above a dry cleaner's on Elysian
Fields, but that was no place to raise kids; they had to cross three
lanes of fast traffic just to play on the neutral ground, and that was-
n't safe even in the daytime. She moved into a narrow little house
with a yard on Dauphine, and they were all happy there until their
next-door neighbor got shot to death on his front porch in broad
daylight. That was when Rosalie decided they were moving to the
suburbs. She'd been out here nearly two years now, and it still felt
like cowtown. Chris, her twelve-year-old, had adjusted all right, but
sixteen-year-old Tommy hated it.

"How 'bout dem spatulas?" said Alice. "You seen 'em anywhere?"

Rosalie started laughing.

"What?" said Alice, a little peeved.

"Nothing, just the way you said that ... *How 'bout dem spatulas* ...
sounded like you were talking about a sports team or something.
Don't mind me," Rosalie said as Alice stared at her. "Chris is so
excited about the Saints game tomorrow, it's all I been hearing. Poor
kid thinks I'm torturing him, making him go to the Mass
and procession instead of stay home and watch football on TV.

Amazing what qualifies as torture to a twelve-year-old, huh?"

"Twelve, hell, my husband thinks the same thing. I don't watch him, he gonna be sitting in the pew with earphones on, waiting for the kickoff."

"Damn, you can't blame him for that," said a voice behind the women. "I mean, the first regular season game and all." Rosalie turned and saw her brother standing at the back of the tent holding a foil-wrapped hotel pan. When he started working in restaurant kitchens more than a decade ago, he had acquired the nickname G-man, but she'd never been able to think of him as anything but Gary. He was the baby of the family, always a calm, sweet-natured kid. Rosalie was the next-youngest, and not nearly so untroubled.

Back when she first met Jamie, the man who was now her ex-husband, Rosalie had believed that all six of the Stubbs children had good instincts. The girls were wholly self-preserving. The boys' only self-destructive trait was a tendency to fall suddenly, tenaciously in love and to pursue the object of their affection whether it proved good for them or not. Otherwise they were as stolid and sane as their sisters. After the divorce, she still thought herself self-preserving, given that she was certain her marriage would have killed her if she'd stayed in it. But she was no longer so sure of her instincts.

Gary set down the hotel pan so Rosalie could give him a hug. His shoulders and back felt bony through the thin cloth of his T-shirt. He was the only one in the family who'd inherited their father's lean Irish build; their mother had been a Bonano before she married, and the other five kids were stocky Sicilians like her.

"You saving our lives bringing this eggplant," Rosalie said. "Otherwise everybody's just gonna hafta eat me and Alice's cooking."

"Aw, you just about taught me to cook," he said for Alice's benefit. It was technically true, but he'd soon displayed more of a talent than Rosalie ever would.

"Move it over here for me, babe. I'm gonna put it on the Sterno in a minute."

"Hey Rosalie," Gary said in a quieter voice, "you seeing anybody?"

She swatted at him. "Yeah, right."

"No, seriously. Guy I know asked about you—saw you and the kids last time y'all ate at the restaurant."

"Who? A cook?"

"Course he's not a cook," Gary said indignantly. "I wouldn't introduce you to a *cook*. What, you think I want my sister living a life of poverty and degeneracy? Mark's a wine salesman. Makes good money, and he's a real nice guy, else I wouldn't be telling you about him."

"Well, I appreciate it, hon, but I'm not interested. I got enough to worry about working at Dillard's and raising these kids. I don't have time to bother with any nice guys."

"Don't have time, or you don't really believe they're out there? Cause they are, I promise. They don't all go chasing after anything that waves a tail at 'em." *Like Jamie*, was the unspoken conclusion of that sentence, but Gary was too kind to say it.

"Listen ... " Rosalie pulled her brother aside and kissed him on the cheek. "I'm happy *you* got a nice guy, OK? No matter what Momma ever says about it, and no matter what you think the Church says, I'm real happy for you and Rickey. I always have been. *But I'm not looking.* Y'all gotta understand that and quit trying to fix me up." Every week, it seemed like, her sister or one of her brothers tried to introduce her to some man. Invariably he was a "real nice guy," and invariably Rosalie declined to meet him.

"Awright, awright," said Gary, who could take a hint better than some of their siblings. "I promised I'd give you his card, though. You can just throw it out if you want." He pulled his wallet from a side pocket of his houndstooth chef pants and riffled through it until he found a business card. Rosalie accepted it between the tips of her forefinger and thumb, as if she were handling something nasty.

Mark Charbonnet, the card read. *Wines Galore and More.* There were two local phone numbers, a fax, and an e-mail address. People had so many ways of making themselves available these days, Rosalie marveled. "What's the 'and more'?"

"Liqueurs, specialty products, all kinda shit. That's what we mostly get from him. You know Rickey hates wine—we got the worst list in the city. Which reminds me, I better get back over there."

"Your brother's real cute," Alice Cannizzaro observed when Gary had gone. "He married?"

"What do you care, you old grammaw?"

"I got a little niece about the right age."

"Well, he's married, or close as you can get," said Rosalie, exasperated. Why was everybody always trying to stick their nose in someone else's business? For that matter, why did everybody have to be paired off anyway? She and the kids did just fine on their own—a hell of a lot better than when Jamie was in the picture.

Things had been all right until she had to have the hysterectomy after Chris was born. The first days following the surgery she spent in the heavenly embrace of the morphine pump, and never even realized Jamie wasn't at the hospital. Once she was home in her own bed, trying to reconcile herself to a new body that didn't look or feel or even *smell* like the one she remembered, it soon became obvious that something was wrong. She could believe he was sleeping on the couch because he was afraid of hurting her. Growing up with four brothers had inoculated her against the stereotype that men are babies about their own pain, but she knew they were often terrified by the pain of others. Even when the scar had faded to a shiny pink smile across her lower belly, though, Jamie didn't really return to her. Before, he had loved spending evenings at home, playing with the kids and sometimes polishing off a six-pack. After the surgery he spent most of his evenings barhopping with his buddies from work, came home smelling of smoke and strange perfume.

"I know it's stupid," he admitted when she tried to talk to him about it. "It's just like ... you had something cut out of there."

"I *did* have something cut out of there," said Rosalie. "Remember? The gynecologist said if I got pregnant again, I could bleed to death. What, Jamie—you'd rather have a whole woman who might die on you than one who doesn't have a uterus, but can live to raise the kids you already got?"

"I know it's stupid," he repeated. But he didn't touch her again, and the barhopping didn't stop. Counseling was not an option; they couldn't afford a professional marriage counselor and Jamie said the priest would only make him feel guilty. Rosalie lay awake late at night, alone in her unwomaned bed, thinking about the gun on the top shelf of the bedroom closet, the Drano under the sink, the pills in the medicine cabinet. But suicide was a mortal sin, far worse than divorce. She would burn in Hell and her boys would grow up motherless. If she could have ensured that they would be raised by her parents or her sister Mary Louise, she might have taken her chances on Hell, but she couldn't stand the thought of them making their way through the world with only their weak-stomached father to protect them.

She and Alice finished setting up the food and decorated the table with some raw artichokes, some lemons and onions, a big cucuzza squash, garlands of crepe paper in red, green, and white, the colors of the Italian flag. The festival was preparing to swing into action. She could hear the band tuning up over on the Rivertown square, could see early arrivals prowling around the food area or waiting for the meal ticket booth to open. She glanced at the sky, which was gray and pregnant-looking. "We gonna get wet before the day's over," she told Alice.

"It always rains right before the St. Rosalie procession," Alice said. "Father heard some people crying about it last year and told 'em the rain come to wash our sins away."

"Well, let it rain then, huh?"

"Yeah, you right."

Rosalie's younger son, Chris, had been wandering around the area with his friend Butch. Now they came running up to the tent, talking over each other with an urgency common to twelve-year-olds everywhere. "MomMA—I gotta get ten dollars—"

"Miz Stubbs, if you loan me a couple bucks, I promise I'll get my daddy to pay you back later—"

"It's real important—"

"Hush!" she said. The boys did, looking up at her expectantly, their eyes very large in their little faces. Each of them held a wad of some kind of white modeling clay they were working between their fingers, stretching and rolling the stuff without seeming to pay much attention to what they were doing. "What's so important you gotta have ten more dollars all of a sudden? You already got your meal tickets. You didn't lose them, did you?"

"No, but Billy Schiro's got a booth over by the Saints museum. He's selling autographed pictures for five bucks a pop."

Billy Schiro was a Saints running back who had retired last year under a discreet cloud of scandal. Nothing had been proven, but there was talk of expensive call girls and cocaine; his wife had left him, taking their three kids and reportedly cleaning up in a nasty divorce. "What you want a picture of that bum for?" Rosalie asked.

"Aw, Momma, he was great, I got his jersey and everything—"

"Yeah, I know—it cost me forty-five dollars last Christmas. I'm not spending any more money on that bum. What happened to the ten dollars I already gave you? You spent it on that stuff?" She indicated the modeling clay in the boys' hands.

"Nuh-uh, they giving this away from the Children's Castle, it was free. We just got a couple ice creams, is all. Please, Momma—"

"*Absolutely not!*" she snapped. Chris eyed her once more and saw that she meant it. He made as if to sulk, but she stared him down until his eyes dropped.

"C'mon," he said to Butch, turning away. "She ain't playing. To hell with Schiro anyway—remember when he dropped that touchdown pass against the Rams last year?" The *hell* was carefully enunciated just loud enough for Rosalie to hear, but she didn't holler after him. When it came to twelve-year-olds, you had to choose your battles.

"Doesn't this stuff look like Roman candy?" said Butch, stretching his handful of clay as they strolled off.

"Dude, it could be way cooler than Roman candy, it could be, like, plastique—"

Rosalie sighed. Probably she had overreacted, but she'd never cared for Billy Schiro. "Selling autographed pictures to kids," she said to Alice. "Just about what I'd expect from a bum like that."

"You said it, girl," Alice replied, but she looked at Rosalie as if she thought the younger woman might start hurling artichokes at passersby. "Why don't you sit down a minute? We got it all set up now."

The rain finally let go when the festival was well underway, forcing people to run under the food tents for cover. Rosalie and Alice's tent sheltered a young woman and a toddler who was making messy work of a meatball cone, a delicacy exclusive to Kenner as far as Rosalie knew: a big meatball plopped into an ice cream cone, doused with red gravy, and topped with Parmesan. The little girl had managed to get some of the meatball in her mouth, but most of the red gravy was in her hair, on her hands, and down the front of her dress. "Lemme clean her up some," said Rosalie, taking a damp napkin and going after the girl's face as the young mother tried to hold the squirming little body still. The kid grinned up at Rosalie, who felt her heart twist. She worshiped her boys—she would die for them if it came to that—but she'd always secretly hoped for a girl. Well, *wish in one hand and spit in the other*, as her mother sometimes said, *and see which one fills up first*.

Sunday dawned cloudy and close, and by the time Rosalie arrived at the church, the air felt like wet gauze. Chris ran over to some friends and started speculating about the outcome of today's football game. He rejoined her inside just as the schoolchildren were beginning their play about the life of St. Rosalie.

"From the time Rosalie was very young, she despised worldly vanities," the sixth-grade narrator recited as the girl playing the saint illustrated this by turning her back on a boy holding a plastic mirror. "When her remarkable beauty caused her hand to be sought in marriage by several lords of Sicily"—the lords filed onto the stage tugging at their robes—"the Blessed Virgin appeared to her and told her to forsake society and its temptations." The Blessed Virgin failed to appear, and there were giggles from the lords as the narrator paused. Then the Virgin rushed out and gestured imperiously at St. Rosalie, who ducked into a paper-mache grotto near the altar. "She obeyed, taking with her only a crucifix. Later she migrated to a grotto on Mount Pellegrino. There she died, and a stalagmite grew over her remains. On the grotto wall she had carved an inscription: *I, Rosalie, daughter of Sinibald, lord of Quis … Quisquina and Rosae, decided to live in this cave for the love of my Lord Jesus Christ.*"

The narrator permitted herself a little sigh of relief; she'd gotten through most of the big words. "In 1624, plague broke out at Palermo. A vision of St. Rosalie appeared to one of the victims." One of the lords returned clutching at his stomach, dressed in rags that had been concealed under his robe. The saint emerged from the grotto holding a cardboard cross and a plastic Halloween skull. "She told the man to find her relics and she would save Palermo from the plague. A search was made and the bones of the maiden were found along with a crucifix, a silver cross, and a rosary. They were put into a reliquary and carried in procession through the city. The plague never returned to Palermo."

More children straggled out holding aloft the various relics (but no bones), looking more like a ragtag second-line parade than a holy procession.

"St. Rosalie is always depicted holding a cross to symbolize her great love for Our Lord Jesus Christ and a human skull to remind us of mortality," the narrator concluded in a businesslike tone. "Her feast day is celebrated every year in Sicily, and we celebrate it here today."

Chris leaned over and poked Rosalie in the upper arm. "That girl is a major brown-nose," he whispered.

Rosalie extended a forefinger and poked him back, but her eyes were fixed on the statue of St. Rosalie that the church deacons had just carried out and placed next to the altar. The statue was about three feet tall, crowned with a wreath of flowers and a gold tiara like a hand-me-down from some Mardi Gras queen, garlanded with ribbons of purple and yellow, pink and green, white and scarlet. The saint's face was handsome rather than pretty, slightly hook-nosed, stern in its hermitical zeal. In one hand she held the cross, in the other the skull.

"What's the skull for again?" an old woman from another pew whispered in a cigarette-hoarse voice.

"Mawtality," said the even older woman beside her.

The Mass went by quickly. Rosalie didn't take Holy Communion at the end; she hadn't had it since her divorce was final. The priest had told her she could resume it when she felt comfortable, but so far the time had not seemed right. The bearers hoisted the statue on its platform and bore it out of the church, and the parishioners followed. Everyone milled around for a few minutes until Father pulled up in a sound truck. "Please take out your rosaries and pray along with me during the procession," he said through a whine of feedback. "If you don't have your rosaries, pray along anyway. There'll be water and Gatorade at several spots along our route. If you'd like to have a prayer said for someone special, let one of the deacons know. Let's go, folks!"

He began a Hail Mary as a little brass band began to play. The procession moved out and began bobbing along the street: a police car, three members of the St. Rosalie Society bearing a cross and two gold candle holders, two more waving an Italian flag and a St. Rosalie banner, the band, the statue with its bearers, and the congregation filing along behind. The sound truck brought up the rear, Father and the deacons pounding out the first part of the prayer—"Hail Mary, full of grace, the Lord is with thee; blessed art Thou among women, and blessed is the fruit of Thy womb Jesus"—and the congregation making the response: "Holy Mary, Mother of God, pray for us sinners now and at the hour of our death, amen." Rosalie had the little white rosary her mother had given her at her first Communion, and Chris had a similar one she had given him, though she noticed that he wasn't even mouthing the words to the prayer.

The procession rounded the corner of Short Street and Williams Boulevard. Rosalie saw Alice Cannizzaro limping along up ahead. Alice was a member of the St. Rosalie Society that decorated and crowned the statue each year. Rosalie herself had been to the Italian-American Heritage Festival many times over the years, but she'd never attended the St. Rosalie Mass or procession until she moved out here, even though she had been named for the saint. "Why Rosalie?" she'd once asked her mother with something approaching distaste. "All she did was sit in a cave and pray." Now it seemed apt, almost cruelly so. But her mother couldn't have known she would marry a man who would reject her in such a way as to make her feel unfit for any other man's love ... and what did that have to do with St. Rosalie anyway? *She* hadn't let any man hurt her; she had disappeared into her cave before any had the chance.

As the procession followed a set of railroad tracks that ran alongside a shallow canal, the air seemed to mold itself to Rosalie's face. Someone had recently mowed grass near here, and the smell was almost sickeningly fresh, like afterbirth. No, it wasn't anything like afterbirth; what was wrong with her? She looped her rosary over one hand and fanned herself with the other. Now the procession was drawing to a halt: they had reached the first water stop. Little paper cups of Kentwood water were arranged on a card table, and a Boy Scout stood by with a garbage bag to collect the empties. Chris handed her a cup and she drank it down gratefully. It was cold and faintly sweet.

"Y'all can take this chance to venerate the statue of St. Rosalie if you like," the priest said through the loudspeaker. People began to approach the statue, touching their rosaries to its base, planting kisses on their hands and stroking its feet. The bearers held the platform steady, looking away so that people could make their devotions in semiprivacy. Rosalie stepped up behind a young man in a black and gold Saints jersey who was bending to press his forehead to the hem of the statue's robe. When he moved away, she put her hand on the platform and looked up into the saint's face. The crown of white flowers had begun to curl and wilt in the heat. The painted eyes gazed back at her. The imperious nose and perfectly arched brows seemed to mock her own sweaty face. *She wouldn't have really looked that good,* Rosalie thought, *not after a few years in that cave. Her cheeks would have sunk, her lips would have cracked. She wouldn't have had to worry about all those suitors anymore—they wouldn't have wanted her once she came out.* Then she looked away, ashamed of her thoughts. When had she become so bitter, so cracked and dried herself?

"Momma." Chris was beside her, tugging her away from the statue. "Mr. Cannizzaro's got the game on a Walkman. He says I can listen to it if I walk with them and help Miz Cannizzaro—her foot hurts. Can I?"

Rosalie looked at him. He was already a handsome kid, with her dark coloring and Jamie's good bone structure. She wondered who he would grow up to hurt. Then she winced at her ugly thoughts and bit the inside of her cheek until her eyes watered.

"Momma?" Now Chris sounded a little alarmed. "You OK?"

"Yeah, baby." She reached out and touched his hair. "Go on ahead. Momma's gonna stay back here for a while."

"Cool, thanks!" He was gone, racing off toward the tinny sound of the football game in Mr. Cannizzaro's earphones. As the procession began to move again, Rosalie took up the prayer. "Hail Mary, full of grace ..." In her own graceless mouth, though, the words offered little comfort. She kept saying them anyway. That was what so many people couldn't understand about being Catholic; the prayers didn't always help, but you just had to keep saying them anyway.

They arrived home late that evening. Chris was cranky because the game had gone into overtime and Mr. Cannizzaro had taken his earphones back. Tommy didn't help matters by gloating over how exciting it had been to see the Saints win in OT. Rosalie fixed a quick dinner—bucatoni with some of the red gravy she kept in individual-sized Tupperwares in the freezer—and sent them both off to bed. Her feet and her hips hurt, and she decided to take a hot bath before going to bed herself. If she could soak out some of the soreness now, it would be easier to stand at the cash register for eight hours tomorrow.

Chris had used up her bubble bath, so she added a dollop of shampoo to the running water. It foamed up nicely enough when you didn't have the real thing. As she undressed, her eye was caught by a messy little scatter of items she'd left on the back of the toilet tank last night. A couple of unused meal tickets from the festival.

A button she'd been embarrassed to wear—it said I'M NOT JUST PERFECT, I'M ITALIAN. The crumpled paper napkin she'd used to wipe the face of the little girl eating the meatball cone. Why had she stuck that dirty thing back in her pocket? Frowning, she pinched it between two fingers and tossed it into the wastebasket. Beneath it was another object: the business card her brother had given her. She could have sworn she'd thrown that away.

She picked up the card and read it again. *Mark Charbonnet. Wines Galore and More.* And all those phone numbers, pager numbers, fax, e-mail. Why would a person make himself so available, she wondered, when there were so many ways to be rejected?

Maybe everyone didn't think like that. Maybe everyone didn't live in a cave.

Rosalie almost pitched the card into the wastebasket, then looked at it again. It seemed like a classy thing to have, a business card. Jamie had worked in the shipping department of a sportswear factory; she supposed guys who drove forklifts didn't need cards. She turned it over. Written in a neat hand was a message she hadn't noticed before: *Please call.*

Without quite knowing why, she lifted the card to her face and breathed its scent: clean and faintly spicy, like an expensive bottle of wine sitting on a fresh linen tablecloth. The smell of another world.

Rosalie laid the card back on the toilet tank and stepped into her bath. It was rare for anything to sit around the house for more than a day without the boys messing it up. Probably tomorrow Chris would throw a T-shirt over the tank or Tommy would lift the top to fiddle with the flush mechanism, which didn't always work. The card would get lost, and she would forget about Mark Charbonnet. That would be the sensible thing to do. She didn't even know what he looked like. Gary had said he was a nice guy, but Gary was so sweet-natured that almost everybody was nice to him. It would be better if the card got lost.

If it didn't, though ... well, then maybe she'd turn it over and read the message again. *Please call.* Maybe she'd let herself breathe that spicy scent one more time.

Rosalie settled into her bath and ducked her head under the water. When she came back up, the bubbles clinging to her dark hair looked almost like a crown of flowers.

Four Flies and a Swatter

There are few things bleaker than a French Quarter bar the day after Mardi Gras. This is actually a cleaner day than usual in New Orleans; police clear the streets at midnight, and crews roll out to shovel tons of garbage (a measure of the annual celebration's success; yearly estimates range from 1200 to 1600 tons). Business owners hose down their sidewalks with bleach. So things smell a little better than average, but everyone is tired of drinking, and the bartenders themselves are near-giddy with exhaustion. They are also, to put it kindly, not the cream of the bartending crop: the cream works Fat Tuesday and gets Wednesday off.

The bar in question was a nameless place on Burgundy, far from the hustle and flash of Bourbon Street. Beyond a few framed pictures of football players, an extravagantly fake Tiffany lightshade, and a pair of neon beer signs, it had no atmosphere to speak of. On this Wednesday evening in 1994 it was occupied by five souls, possibly lost ones, but at least they'd gotten through another Carnival season. Two men in cook's whites and check pants sat at a corner table drinking beer. The older one, thirty or so, had a smudge of ash on his forehead that had faded considerably over the course of a long kitchen shift, but which he had somehow avoided wiping or sweating off. The younger cook's brow was ash-free. A few tables away, a man in early middle age sat sipping well-brand Scotch with ice. He had a battered fedora he did not wear on his head, but only turned over and over in his hard brown hands, sometimes pinching around the brim as if he were making a pie crust, occasionally folding it right in half.

The fourth customer sat at the bar, his elbows propped on the shiny wood, his hands cupped around a glass of beer. Upon entering the bar, he had asked for a Hurricane, instantly marking himself as a tourist. "We don't have that," the bartender told him. "That's Bourbon Street stuff."

"Hand Grenade?" the tourist had asked.

"Bourbon Street stuff."

"Daiquiri?"

Silently, the bartender shook his head.

"Bourbon just two blocks over," the man with the fedora called across the room. "They sell you all that shit, charge you a arm and a leg and prob'ly your dick too."

The tourist looked over and smiled uncomfortably, but the bartender ignored the man. "We got regular drinks. All the usual stuff. Beer on tap—Bud, Abita, Dixie."

"I'll take a Dixie," the tourist decided.

"Course he will," the young cook muttered to the other. "It's got the most *local color.*" The older cook stifled a laugh, but said nothing.

The bartender himself was of middling height, indeterminate age, and the pallid complexion of a white man with a night job; his most distinguishing characteristic was his strong New Orleans accent. The speech of all the drinkers (except the tourist) left no doubt that they were locals, but the bartender had one of those voices that seems to have been dragged along the Mississippi River bottom, picking up sand, grit, broken glass, and possibly a few rusty nails. The cooks and the fedora-worrier thought nothing of it, but the tourist's ears hurt a little every time the bartender spoke.

Though he wasn't fast enough to work Fat Tuesday, he wasn't a bad bartender. Despite his brush-off of Hurricanes and Hand Grenades as "Bourbon Street stuff," he understood that the tourist was looking for some sort of authentic New Orleans experience. Tourists almost always were, and the harder they looked, the farther away from it they got. Now, however, he remembered something. He groped underneath the bar and found what he'd hidden there two days ago, back behind a lowboy refrigerator that held half-and-half, grapefruit juice, and other seldom-used mixers. "Hey, you buncha drunks, check this out," he said. "Somebody left this here on Monday, still sealed up and everything. Never came back for it. Whaddaya say we crack it open?"

He held up a tall bottle with a picture of four green flies on its crudely printed label. When he'd found and hidden the bottle, he had thought the label depicted butterflies or beetles, but now he saw that the insects were definitely flies—the hard-headed, hairy-legged kind that buzzed around the garbage when it wasn't picked up on time. In the glow of the beer signs, the bottle's contents were a lurid, toxic-looking green.

"What is it?" said the tourist.

The bartender turned the label toward him and read it aloud. "Four Flies Absinthe. One hundred forty proof. Product of Croatia."

"A hundred forty proof?" said the younger cook. "Shit!"

"Absinthe," said the man with the fedora, as if the word had flipped some switch in his mind. "Jean Lafitte imported it. Voodoo queen used to buy it off him for parties."

"I thought absinthe came from France," said the tourist.

"Not this bottle, I guess." The bartender put his hand on the twist-off metal cap. "So whaddaya say? You guys wanna have our own little party?"

"Ain't that stuff illegal?" said the older cook. "You oughtn'ta open it if it's illegal. You could lose your license."

"Who's gonna tell?"

"Well, I don't know. Cops could walk in here any minute."

"Aw, they all too tired to bother us. And I guarantee my owner's gonna be passed out in bed for the next two days. How about it?" The bartender eyed the older cook. "You look like a guy who likes a nice strong drink. Wanna shot of this? It's on me."

"Nah, man, no thanks." The cook waved a dismissive, burn-scarred hand. "I gave up drinking for Lent."

This struck everyone momentarily speechless, and they all sat staring at him. Finally the younger cook said, "Anthony, what the hell you mean you gave up drinking for Lent? You're sitting in a bar drinking beer right now."

"Beer ain't really drinking. I just drink a couple beers to relax. I gave up liquor, though."

The younger cook sat shaking his head, and the bartender appealed to him. "What about you, kid? I bet you'd like a little something stronger than that beer."

"No thanks. I heard absinthe tastes like Herbsaint, Pernod, all that anise shit. It's gross."

"*Gross*? What are you, chicken?" said the bartender, who was starting to get a little annoyed.

"Hey, fuck you, pal. Gimme a shot of Wild Turkey 101, I'll drink it. I'm just not drinking something that's a hundred forty proof and tastes like a cross between licorice and roach bait."

"It might taste bad," said the man who had now abandoned his fedora on the table, "but you know what? There's a story behind it. I'm tellin you, the pirate Jean Lafitte used to run absinthe through the swamps south of here and sell it to Marie Laveau for her voodoo parties. They'd all be drinkin that shit over in St. Louis Cemetery, dancin on the graves, puttin snakes around their necks and ... well, let's just say their necks wasn't the only place they put 'em. Once in a while Jean Lafitte save a bottle for himself, drink it with Andrew Jackson on the balcony of the Cornstalk Fence Hotel."

"Hey, wait a minute!" said the tourist. "I heard that story before! Don't you drive one of those tour buggies? Sure, I remember you. Your mule wears a hat with pink peonies on it."

"Sure enough," said the fedora man, squinting at the tourist. "Come to think of it, I remember you too. You a lousy tipper."

"I figured he was a buggy driver," said the younger cook to the older one. "They can't tell any story about New Orleans without putting either Jean Lafitte or Elvis in it."

"I didn't know you were supposed to tip," the tourist said apologetically. "Once I paid for the buggy ride, I only had five bucks left over."

"Yeah, five bucks you wasn't gonna spend on motherfuckin Hurricanes and Hand Grenades—"

"Hey, no language, no fighting," said the bartender. "Jeez, I don't believe you people. Try to give you a free drink and all you can do is bitch. What about you?" He set a clean glass in front of the tourist. "C'mon, Cap, put these locals to shame. Have a shot of absinthe on me."

"Well, I don't think you're supposed to drink it by the *shot*," said the tourist. He still sounded apologetic, but he seemed to be gaining courage. "There's supposed to be a special glass and spoon, and you have to filter it through a sugar cube and mix it with ice water—"

"OK. OK, you know what? *Fuck this!*" The bartender had not worked Fat Tuesday, but he'd had more than his share of hours during the past two weeks. Since he was not particularly fast, he had received poor tips compared to his coworkers. All this had put him in a nasty mood, from which he'd been trying to recover by sharing his contraband bottle with these straggling drinkers. Now he picked it up by the neck, walked to the door, and sent it sailing out into Burgundy Street, where it smashed on the opposite sidewalk.

"Yo, time to get moving," said the younger cook. "Come on, Anthony, I gotta go home anyway—G said he might get off early tonight." The cooks got up from their table and exited the bar, leaving their round of beers half-finished. They were far too tired to get into a bar fight.

"Guess I'll make like a banana and split, too," said the buggy driver. He plucked his fedora from the table, settled it carefully on his head, and left without sparing the bartender even a final, contemptuous glance.

"Sorry," said the tourist. "I've been in New Orleans a week, but this is the first time I've been anywhere near sober. I don't really know how to act."

"Aw, forget it," said the bartender. "Stuff prob'ly tasted like crap anyway. Lemme buy you another beer."

Outside, the green liquid trickled across the sidewalk and soaked into the cracks, mingling with the French Quarter grime and gruel. It had never seen the inside of a distillery; it had been brewed in a very small batch by four Croatian kids. They had a slick little printing press on which they'd made the label, but they knew no better than to fortify their product with highly toxic oil of wormwood. Two of the kids had died after sampling their own product. The other two only suffered massive brain damage.

The Zagreb police confiscated the remainder of the absinthe to be destroyed, but all four bottles were stolen from the evidence room by a rookie who didn't know its history. He sent the bottles to his niece in New York, who frequented goth clubs and had written innumerable letters begging him to find her some. The package made it through U.S. Customs, but two of the bottles cracked in transit and arrived worthless. The niece put one away for a special occasion and gave one to her college roommate, who was going to New Orleans for Mardi Gras. The roommate had been terribly peeved to lose the bottle, but that was just the sort of thing that happened at Carnival.

Henry Goes Shopping

Henry Stubbs approaches the cash register at the K&B drugstore on Canal Street, a tall, honest-faced young man with a thick shock of black hair inherited from his Italian mother. He lives in another part of New Orleans, farther downtown with his parents even though he is now nineteen, gainfully employed, and fairly bursting to be out on his own, but he has deliberately stopped off here to do his shopping. He'd hate to run into any member of his family just now. In his purple shopping basket are four items, all of which have some association with his girlfriend, Leonetta: a can of shaving cream, a roll of breath mints, a bottle of aspirin, and a box of condoms.

The shaving cream is because Leonetta has delicate skin, Uptown skin, and she says Henry's face scratches her. He has always shaved the way his father and older brothers taught him, with plain old soap and water, but he is willing to try the store-bought kind to protect Leonetta's delicate Uptown skin. The breath mints are self-explanatory. The aspirin is because, as much as he loves Leonetta, she can give him a powerful headache sometimes. The condoms are because he's been sleeping with her for a month and a half

now—twelve times, which has used up their first box of condoms—
and that is worth any number of headaches.

There's a long line at the register, as there almost always is during the Christmas season, and Henry has already fallen in before he
notices that the person in front of him is a nun. Her dark blue habit
is pinned to the top of her gray head, which isn't much higher than
Henry's waist. In her cart he can see a number of sparkly Christmas
ornaments shaped like gingerbread cottages and such, a plastic dish
made to resemble cut glass, and a big package of adult diapers. He
is trying not to think about the diapers—shouldn't such things be
provided for elderly nuns, or is she maybe taking care of someone
else?—when he remembers the condoms in his own basket. His
heart sinks in his chest. He glances hopefully at the other register,
even feints toward it a little, but the girl counting money there gives
him a frosty stare and says, "This one closed."

All the Stubbs children—four boys and two girls—were required
to make First Communions, to be confirmed, and to attend Mass
twice a week until they were thirteen. Their father is medium-
devout, their mother extremely so, but even she wasn't up to the
task of forcing six teenagers to attend Mass on a regular basis, and
after thirteen the matter of their faith was more or less left up to
them. Henry has not attended many Masses since reaching the age
of emancipation, but the beliefs of the Catholic Church—and particularly a near-superstitious reverence for priests and nuns—is
deeply ingrained in him. His parents could not afford to send him
to a Catholic school, so he isn't precisely *afraid* of nuns, but the
thought of having one see him buy contraceptives is nevertheless
appalling. For one absurd instant he thinks of not getting the condoms, of surreptitiously slipping them onto the shelf of candy and
other impulse items near the registers, but that would be a bad idea:

he's meeting Leonetta tonight and she will expect him to have them. She likes the sex as much as he does, seems almost ravenous for it; the only time she ever drops the snooty Uptown demeanor she has cultivated for God knows how long is when he's actually on top of her, inside her, fucking her. Her hunger for it excites Henry as much as the actual sensations. No, he can't put the condoms back.

Instead he puts the shopping basket behind his back, but that seems silly and likely to call attention to himself, so he holds it normally and just wills the nun not to turn and look at him. She's examining the merchandise on the impulse shelves: cigarette lighters, mass-produced pralines, a cassette tape of New Orleans-themed Christmas songs by a local band called Ya Momma'n'Em. Henry can see one bright eye scanning the items. Just as he begins to fear his scrutiny will attract her attention and rolls his eyes ceilingward, she looks up at him, cocks her head, and speaks in a high, hoarse voice: "Say, babe, you ever heard this record?"

He's still pondering the likelihood of a nun calling him *babe* when he realizes her question requires a response. "Uh, yeah," he says, and then fakes a cough and clears his throat. "Scuse me, I mean, yes, Sister, I heard it. My dad has a copy he plays in his car sometimes. It's pretty funny." He tries to hold her gaze, certain that if he doesn't, his own eyes will go straight to his basket and drag hers with them.

"They want four-ninety-nine for it, though, huh? That seems kinda high."

Nuns take a vow of poverty, Henry remembers. He wonders if he should offer to buy it for her. No, that would be presumptuous if not actually rude. "It does seem a little high," he says lamely.

"Well, maybe I'll get me one next time," she says. It's her turn to pay now, and she begins transferring her items onto the counter, starting with the sparkly Christmas ornaments and ending with the adult diapers. It takes her a few minutes to pry the exact change out of her little coin purse, but finally she finishes. "You have a nice Christmas, now," she says to him as she leaves. "I'm gonna get that record next time."

"Merry Christmas to you, Sister," he manages, feeling an obscure sense of reprieve.

The cashier rings up his items without comment or apparent judgment. The first time Henry bought condoms he felt a mingled sense of embarrassment and pride, but now it seems routine. His chagrin at the nun's presence is already nearly forgotten. He wonders if sex with Leonetta will eventually become routine too, hopes not. He pays with a twenty-dollar bill and exits onto Canal Street. The December air is cold and, for New Orleans, even a little crisp. He climbs into his old beater and heads downtown, a young man with sex in his immediate future and all the possibilities of life ahead of him, mercifully unaware of whatever sorrows the years ahead may hold.

The Working Slob's Prayer
(Being a night in the history of the Peychaud Grill)

Leslie ducked through the swinging doors and approached the pass, setting her feet with care on the slippery tile floor. As always when she entered the kitchen, she could feel its steamy, pungent atmosphere settling onto her skin and permeating the long black braid that hung down her back. By the end of the night she would be filthy despite her best efforts, with food grimed into the sleeves of her shirt and greasing the quicks of her nails.

Beyond the pass, the heart of the kitchen was a cacophony of shouts, clattering pans, hissing water, and sudden jets of flame. "You got my entrees for table 18?" she called over the din. "They say it's been forty minutes."

The chef, Paco Valdeon, glared at her through the curdle of steam that rose off the sauté pan he was holding six inches above the flame. The ropy muscles of his forearm strained not at all as he supported the heavy pan, tattoos rippling and bulging. His slate-gray eyes were flat and hostile. A cigarette dangled from the corner of his mouth, something she'd always thought was just a cliché until she started waiting tables at the Peychaud Grill two weeks ago.

"Confucius say dumbshit who order porterhouse medium-well expect to wait forty minutes," he said. "*At least* forty minutes. I usually tack on fifteen more just as a kind of asshole tax."

"Goddamn it, Chef, I mean, please, Chef, I really need that food. Rickey, can I at least take the lady's fish? She's the one really giving me hell."

The young cook working the hot line next to Chef Paco scowled at her. He was a nice enough guy most of the time, but God forbid he should speak politely to a waitress in front of his chef. "Fish'll be ready when the porterhouse is," he said.

"Jeez, Leslie, just go back and lean over the table for five more minutes." This from Shake, the sous chef, presumably in reference to the extra button undone on Leslie's white Oxford shirt. The other waitresses called it the tip button. "Make the guy forget all about his nasty-ass burnt porterhouse."

Unlike the chef, Rickey and Shake were New Orleans natives, and their hoarse, full-throated accent grated on Leslie's nerves. She was from Brooklyn herself, and the people she'd grown up with sounded positively musical by comparison.

"Yeah, maybe let that black bra strap slide down a li'l bit—"

"Hell, just pop one right out—"

"Fuck you in the ass, pig motherfuckers!" she yelled as loud as she could, which was considerably. No one in the kitchen stopped what he was doing—you couldn't stop when a kitchen was as busy as the Peychaud's was now, not without risking disaster—but there was the briefest suggestion of a shocked pause. "If I want any more shit from you, I'll scrape it off the end of my dick, OK? Now I'm gonna go out there and tell those people five minutes, and I'm gonna come back here in *four* minutes, and I want to see my food in the pass. I don't care if you have to throw the goddamn steak in the fryer. Got it?"

No one answered, but they glanced at her with sullen respect, a couple of them hiding grins.

"Good."

"Damn, Leslie," said G-man, the cook who was working the grill station, "we gonna have to elect you Freak of the Week."

"Dude, we can't make a *waitress* Freak of the Week," said Rickey.

"Not even if she has a dick?"

Ignoring all this, Leslie turned and left the kitchen. All cooks were pigs, and some of them thought waitresses existed to be shit upon, but they could forget about that garbage with a Brooklyn girl.

✝ ✝ ✝

Paco Valdeon had learned to cook in Nancy, a little French town near the German border. In 1980 everything there was sausages and sauerkraut and fondue, but he'd scammed his way into staying with the remnants of a family, a 45-year-old woman and two teenagers who'd just been left high and dry by the man of the house. Well, maybe not precisely dry. Even at twenty Paco wasn't handsome, but he was young and already had the unclean virility of a born head chef. Among other things, Minette had been an excellent cook, and she taught him what was still the most important thing he knew about food: you could enhance ingredients by combining them, sometimes even to the point of culinary magic, but no dish could be better than its ingredients. This was a valuable lesson for a kid whose previous position had been in the pantry of a "gourmet" restaurant in Baltimore, trimming leathery green beans, slicing corky tomatoes, and picking the salvageable bits out of blackened heads of lettuce.

By the time he fetched up in New Orleans seven years later—long enough to break the curse of the hand mirror Minette had thrown at him the night before he left Nancy—he was sustaining himself on cocaine, tequila, and hate. He hated all restaurant diners, most because they couldn't appreciate his food, the rest because they could and thought it gave them some sort of claim on him. He hated all wait staff because they made ridiculous amounts of money for working a tenth as hard as he did. He hated women on general principle, which did not prevent him from fucking them if he could.

At the Peychaud Grill he was as close to content as he'd ever been. Most restaurant owners were clueless assholes, and the Peychaud's was no exception, but at least the guy respected his food and generally stayed out of his way instead of trying to be involved. He'd worked for plenty of people who didn't know a goddamn thing about food, but wanted to tell him how to cook anyway, criticizing his food costs and making him vet every dish with them before it went on the menu. The owner of the Peychaud Grill seemed to spend most of his time betting on horses at the racetrack, and Paco thought that was just dandy. Even so, his contentment did not prevent him from being full of hate. He thrived on hate, would have felt bereft without it.

More than anything, he hated prettyboy chefs. Paco had come up at the very beginning of the celebrity chef craze and fervently believed he had been passed over for several jobs because of his receding hairline, his burgeoning gut, and a pair of ears that would have given Dumbo pinna envy. There were few things he enjoyed more than leafing through the latest trendy chef-driven cookbook, finding gorgeous color pictures of the chef in question and mocking his inevitable square jaw, broad shoulders, or carefully mussed hair. All other things being equal, he himself preferred a crew with obvious defects, such as excess weight, scars, missing teeth, and so forth.

That was the main reason he hadn't wanted to hire Rickey, a seriously good-looking kid with intense blue-green eyes and a grin that belonged in a toothpaste commercial. Rickey's friend and roommate, G-man, Paco's best sauté guy at the time, had had to plead Rickey's case with the skill of a trial lawyer: "Honest to God, Paco, he's the most hardcore cook I know. He never reads anything but cookbooks. He went to the CIA—"

"Fuck that. I'll have to make him unlearn all the bad habits they taught him."

"But he didn't graduate! He got kicked out for beating up a guy."

Embarrassingly, this account of Rickey's exit from cooking school was probably what had made Paco hire him. A few months later, when he finally figured out that Rickey and G-man were more than roommates, it softened the blow a little: anybody who'd gotten kicked out of school for fighting couldn't be all bad. Rickey and G-man were just regular guys, not faggy or P.C. or any of that shit, and after a while he stopped caring what they did when they weren't at work.

In the life of every serious cook, there is a chef who makes him (or her) understand the necessity of caring so deeply about food that you are willing to make enemies over it. For Rickey, that chef was Paco Valdeon.

Rickey had come to the Peychaud Grill because it paid better than his last job and he wanted to work with G-man. Ever since high school, they'd always worked together when they could. Within a week, though, he understood that this job would shape him more profoundly than anything else he had done in his life. He was already a roller; he and G-man had both been rollers since they were sixteen or so. They could handle an unexpected rush without getting in the weeds or putting out inferior plates; they could generate tremendous volumes of food; they even had some experience designing specials. Most valuable of all to anyone smart enough to hire them both, they knew each other's kitchen habits and rhythms intimately, and they worked like two parts of a single organism. Paco Valdeon, though, was the first culinary genius Rickey had ever known. The fact that Paco was also something of a thug didn't bother him a bit; in fact, Rickey, who had grown up in a rough neighborhood, was still young enough to find his thug-gishness part of the draw.

One of his favorite Paco stories was the one about the specialty condiments. Paco had spent some time in California wine country before coming to New Orleans, and at one point when his cook's job wasn't covering all the bills, he'd gone to a bulk grocery store and bought up dozens of gallons of cheap vinegar, mustard, and jelly. He had transferred them into fancy bottles and jars from a local thrift shop, gotten his then-girlfriend to label them in a nice round hand ("Strawberry-Zinfandel Confit"; "Rosemary-Infused Balsamic"), and peddled them to area gift shops at vastly inflated prices. Supposedly he'd cleared more than $500 on the scam, but what Rickey really admired was the way he'd demonstrated that most people had no taste; they would buy anything and call it good as long as somebody charged them enough money.

G-man hadn't liked the condiment story nearly as much as Rickey did.

"Sure, Paco's great," he'd said when Rickey related it, "but what's so cool about ripping off a bunch of people who just wanted to buy something nice? What if they were buying a present for their mom?"

G-man had grown up in a strict Catholic family and still had a touch of the altar boy in him. It infuriated Rickey, particularly when Rickey could kind of see his point.

"Their mom probably thought it was good too," he said sullenly. "If she ever opened it. You know most people just stick that kinda shit in their pantry and think *Oh, I'll have to try that one of these days.*"

"Uh huh."

There was a world of nuance in that *uh huh*, most of it disapproving. Anyway, Paco said he wouldn't repeat the stunt if he had it to do over again; there was enough bad food in the world without spreading it around. Rickey thought that was pretty cool too.

"It's not even sanitary," G-man said a few minutes later.

"Neither is most restaurant cooking. Jeez, drop it, will you?"

This conversation wasn't as hostile as it sounded, since they'd had it while lying in bed, legs entwined, immediately after having sex. This was how they spent much of their time when they weren't at work. They'd only been out of their parents' houses for a few years, and privacy was still a novelty, something they could wallow in. They hadn't yet learned to take each other for granted.

Sometimes, though, G-man worried that he was losing Rickey to the Peychaud Grill. During their previous term of employment at a stodgy old French Quarter hotel restaurant called Reilly's, they had come straight home most nights. Now they usually stayed and partook of whatever debauchery was going on after the dinner shift: prodigious drinking, pot-smoking, lines of cocaine laid out on the long copper bar, boxes of nitrous oxide chargers that whipped cooks' brains instead of cream. G-man enjoyed all this as much as Rickey did, but sometimes he'd look at Rickey through the clouds of smoke and the haze of drunkenness and think, *I wish we could just go home like we used to.*

He never said so, though, because ever since they started working at the Peychaud, Rickey had developed the alarming habit of talking about "fags." By this he did not simply mean men who slept with other men, against whom he obviously had no legitimate beef, but men who whined, bitched, ruined orders, or otherwise displayed some type of weakness. It was a habit he'd picked up from Paco, and one G-man disliked intensely, but he didn't dare say anything to Rickey for fear of being labeled a fag himself. He supposed his mother had been right years ago when she said he cared too much what Rickey thought of him.

"Sure, I'll drop it," he said. "I was just, like, registering as a condiment objector."

Rickey was still kind-hearted enough to laugh at his lame joke, and the little moment of tension passed. Even so, it was never exactly easy being gay in the culture of the kitchen, where your worth was measured by burn scars, where women and fags couldn't hang. At the Peychaud it was even less easy than usual.

When the couple walked in just after eight, the maitre d' pegged them as serious eaters. It wasn't that they were fat or anything—the man was tall and lean, the woman small but rather muscular-looking. It was just an attitude they had, a mixture of anticipation and contempt. Serious eaters were disappointed so often that they kept their contempt just below the surface, ready to pull out at a moment's notice.

"How long have you been open?" the woman asked as the maitre d' seated them.

"Three years."

"Really?" she said as if she doubted his word. "I don't know how we missed you before. We try to keep up with the various openings and closings."

"Well, we're glad you're here now." He pulled out her chair, handed them the menus, unfolded their napkins. "You folks have a good meal."

When the maitre d' had gone, the woman scanned the menu with a practiced eye and said, "Look, Seymour, they have fresh sardines. That's always a good sign."

"Go for them, Doc."

"Well, of course I'm going to go for them. You know I order fresh sardines or anchovies any time I see them on a menu, just on principle. Too many people are frightened of little oily fish. It's important to show the chef your support when he's taking risks."

"He's not taking *too* many risks," said Seymour. "There's that damn oyster and Pernod soup again. I'm getting really tired of seeing that everywhere. If you want to serve oysters Rockefeller, then *serve* oysters Rockefeller. Don't make it into a goddamn *soup*."

"I agree. But he's got to have a few sure-fire items, doesn't he?"

"The artichokes are a nice touch, anyway," said Seymour. "Practically everybody who attempts a facsimile of oysters Rockefeller feels compelled to load it up with spinach. I don't think Antoine's uses spinach in the original version. I think they use artichokes."

"I know, dear. Are you trying to talk yourself into ordering the soup?"

"Good God, no. I'm looking at the foie gras and the grouper. What are you ordering, Doc? Are you going for the osso buco?"

"No, it's served with cauliflower quenelles. You know I can't stand cauliflower."

"Sorry, I forgot. The pork shank, then?"

"I'm thinking about it. Are you having the Creole tomato salad?"

"Maybe. I'm interested in that shaved Vella Dry Jack. Why? Are you?"

"I'm not sure. I'm iffy on the pork shank—I may do three appetizer courses. Can you guess which ones?"

"The sardines, then the salad, then the terrine."

"Precisely."

"Do you think that'll be enough to eat?"

"I'm saving room for dessert," said Doc. "I hear the desserts here are very unusual."

Leslie came and took their drink orders. When she had gone, Doc glanced over the menu again, sighed deeply, and said, "But, you know, I think I really want that pork shank."

"Order in," said Leslie, hanging the ticket in the pass. "Hey, Chef, I think these people at table five might be food writers or something. From what I could hear, they went over every item on the menu."

"Great," said Paco. "Just what I needed tonight. I always like to have food writers in the house when I'm hung over."

"You're always hung over," said Shake.

Paco flipped him off without looking away from the row of tickets, then began to call out the new order. "Rickey, ordering one tomato salad, one terrine."

"One tomato and one terrine, Chef."

"G-man, ordering one sardines, one foie, one grouper."

"One sardines, one foie, one grouper, Chef."

"Shake, ordering one pork shank."

"One pork."

Paco improvised two amuses-bouches of prosciutto, asparagus tips, and Louisiana caviar. "Hey, Leslie," he said as the runner came back in, "take these to the food writers."

"Sure thing, Chef."

Seymour and Doc smiled rather smugly as the waitress placed the complimentary canapés before them. They were used to receiving amuse-bouches and other little perks in the restaurants they frequented, but it was especially nice getting one the first time they ate at a place.

"Lovely," they agreed as they used their salad forks to spear the little packets of air-dried ham and asparagus. They left the salad forks on the canapé plates, nonchalantly sure that new ones would be provided when their first course arrived.

The tomato salad and sardines came to the table a few minutes later. A runner had already cleared the canapé plates and salad forks. Doc raised her eyebrows as Leslie set the plates down and turned away. "Excuse me," she said, a hair louder than was strictly necessary, "may we have some fresh *forks*, please?"

"Of course. Excuse me." Leslie hurried to the wait station, grabbed two salad forks, and delivered them to the table.

"Thank you *very* much," said Doc, smiling up at the younger woman to signal that all was forgiven for now.

"You're welcome. Please let me know if you need anything else."

"I will," Doc said honestly. She cut a sardine in thirds with the side of her fork and put one section in her mouth. "Oh," she moaned as the mingled oiliness of the fish and buttery sour-sweetness of the sauce melted over her tongue. "Oh, that's so good."

"I don't suppose I can have a bite," said Seymour. Instead of answering, Doc just pulled her plate closer and snarled at him. "That's all right," he told her. "I know how you feel about those little oily fish. Anyway, my salad is very nice. I'm glad *someone* can still get tomatoes that taste like tomatoes."

Wanting to draw out the experience of eating the three tangy little fish, Doc put down her fork for a moment. "I *know*," she said. "That heirloom tomato salad I had last week at Bayona tasted of absolutely nothing at *all*."

"Do you want to try this?"

"Yes, please, as long as we're not trading. Don't give me any pickled onions; I don't like them ... "

As Shake broke down his station, scrubbing surfaces and covering what was left of his mise-en-place, he went over the conversation he'd had with his father this morning. He had already been over this conversation ten or twelve times, but he couldn't get it out of his head even though it caused a scary high-pressure sensation in his skull every time he thought of it.

"That restaurant is ruining you," Johnny Vojtaskovic said without preamble, coming into the kitchen as Shake downed his first cup of coffee.

It was hard to defend himself when he knew his eyes were red, his pits stank, and the mug in his hand was trembling slightly but visibly. That was Reason Number One why he really needed to move out of his parents' house: he was sick of making excuses for being a slob. Nonetheless, he said, "I'm fine."

Johnny snorted as he took eggs from the refrigerator, broke them into a skillet, stirred them and sprinkled Vegeta over the top. Shake's parents were native New Orleanians, born and raised in Gentilly Woods, but their Croatian-born parents had used Vegeta in everything; it was the taste of their childhoods. It was the taste of Shake's childhood too, but just now its familiar salty-green aroma made his stomach roll over.

"You know what you look like?" Johnny said, scraping the eggs onto a plate. They were barely cooked, still mucilaginous, the way his father had always liked them.

"I bet you're gonna tell me."

"A bum."

Johnny forked eggs into his mouth. Shake wondered how he could stand to eat the snotty-looking things without toast or salt or anything but goddamn Vegeta. He forced himself to look away; he was going to make himself puke if he didn't watch it. When was he going to learn that he could do cocaine *or* tequila shots, but not cocaine *and* tequila shots? After all, he wasn't Paco.

"Well," he said carefully, "I guess I am kind of a bum. We all are. We're just working slobs."

He thought of a little refrain Paco had taught him, something Paco called the Working Slob's Prayer.

Please God, don't let me fuck anything up tonight.
If I do fuck up, don't let anybody notice.
If somebody notices, don't let them tell my boss.
If they tell my boss, let him be too drunk to give a shit.
Thank you, God, amen.

"That's what I been trying to tell you!" Johnny said excitedly. "You stay in that business, you gonna turn old before your time. Now look, you wanna come on with us, I can start you at ten an hour—"

"I'm *making* ten an hour."

"Ten twenty-five, then. Aw, son, it's breaking your mother's heart to see you throw away your life like this."

Johnny and Lydia Vojtaskovic ran a venerable and popular pest control business; they had been engaged in the Sisyphean task of killing New Orleans roaches since 1953. The hell of it was that Johnny's own parents, like most Croatians in Louisiana, were in the seafood business and had pressured Johnny to follow in their footsteps. Uninterested in oysters, Johnny had sold off the family beds as soon as his folks retired, moved from Plaquemines Parish to New Orleans, and started up his company with the profits. For years he had listened to his father's dire prophecies about how the chemicals would give him cancer, the blacks would shoot him dead in the street, his son would hang around the French Quarter and grow up a fruit. Perhaps because none of this had happened yet, Johnny felt free to nag his own son in exactly the same way.

"I'm not throwing away my life, Dad. I like cooking. I'm probably not ever gonna be a famous chef, but I work in a real good restaurant and I make a decent living."

"Real good restaurant. Ha!" The Vojtaskovics had eaten at the Peychaud Grill once, had pronounced the portions tiny and the prices absurd, and hadn't returned. Shake wondered what it would feel like to know your parents were proud of you.

"Yeah, I'm aware of how you feel, Dad," said Shake, but Johnny had dumped his plate in the sink and was leaving the room.

Thinking now of his father's retreating back, he closed the door of the reach-in cooler a little too hard. "Something wrong, dude?" said G-man, who was breaking down his own station.

"Nah, just family shit."

"Tell me about it."

"Your folks a pain in your ass too?" He had wondered about Rickey and G-man's relationship, but had never asked. It was better not to go looking for information you didn't really want.

"Catholic," said G-man, and didn't elaborate. He didn't need to. On top of everything else, Shake's parents were Catholic too.

"So were those people really food writers or what?" said Paco. Service had been over for thirty minutes, and he was just settling in at the bar while the rest of the crew cleaned up the kitchen. Leslie was trying to sneak past him on her way out, hoping he wouldn't ask her this very question.

"Uh, no," she said sheepishly. "I finally asked them, because, you know, they kept talking about the *composition* of the dishes, and asking where you'd cooked before, and all kinds of shit. But no, they weren't food writers."

"What were they?"

"The guy was a poet. The lady said she was the coroner of Orleans Parish."

Leslie winced, expecting a torrent of abuse. But Paco only shrugged and said, "Well, did they like their meal?"

"Oh, absolutely. They wanted to meet you, but I told them you were swamped."

No matter how busy or slow the restaurant was, Paco Valdeon was invariably too "swamped" to make dining room rounds. Almost as much as prettyboy chefs, he hated chefs who thought half their job consisted of swanning around the dining room taking compliments on the food. He'd known chefs who kept separate, spotless white jackets for just that purpose, and would change into them when they left the line. Paco's own white jackets were stained, frayed at the cuffs, and unmonogrammed. He wasn't opposed to head chefs wearing a discreet monogram of their own name and the restaurant's, but lately it seemed as if a guy couldn't even get a sous chef job without running out and buying four or five brand-new jackets with fancy monograms, cloth-covered buttons, colored piping, and every other frill he could think of. It was like they thought the most important part of being a cook was getting to wear a cool costume.

Paco picked up the first of many tequila shots and tossed it down his throat. The smooth agave burn spread through him, familiar and comforting. Someday, he promised himself, he was going to write a book about all the bullshit he'd seen in his days of kitchen work. All the sordid sex, all the preening vanity, all the filth and corruption. People loved shit like that. He was sure it would be a bestseller.

Crown of Thorns

In the Deep South, Halloween Day is usually shirtsleeve weather. But when the sun begins to sink, there's a foretaste of winter in the air. Pools of shadow deepen and lengthen, and the Alabama hills are transformed into moody tapestries of orange and black.

—Robert R. McCammon,
"He'll Come Knocking at Your Door"

The soil of a man's heart is stonier.

—Stephen King, *Pet Sematary*

Hank was arranging an artistic display of squash, pumpkins, and Indian corn when he saw Dr. Brite coming through the big glass doors at the front of the market. Though it was well past Labor Day, the doctor wore a light blue seersucker suit, slightly rumpled. Only if you knew to look for them would you notice the tiny smears and pinpoints of blood on the pants cuffs. The doctor didn't perform autopsies in his street clothes, of course, but he did have a bad habit of walking around the morgue in them, and the floors were far from clean. He always carried the faintest scent of death with him like traces of the devil's own fabric softener.

The doctor reached Hank and stood before him, rocking back slightly on the heels on his expensive but scuffed penny loafers. The loafers weren't bloody, as morgue personnel were required to wear shoe covers at all times. Dr. Brite had made that rule himself. "So we won't be tracking bits of Paw-Paw or Shontell all over New Orleans," he'd said once, trying to shock Hank. He was a middle-aged person of sleek but gloomy aspect: silver temples, incipient jowls, slight potbelly due to his great love of all things culinary. Hank couldn't imagine why he had fallen in love with this man. He'd never even been with a man before, but he couldn't deny the powerful charge of eroticism between them although he knew the doctor thought of him as little more than a boy toy, slightly more sentient than the bodies on his tables. Dr. Brite was still in love with Seymour, his so-called husband, an insufferable-sounding poet who'd left him nearly two years ago.

Well, the sex was good, anyway, and the doctor knew a lot of chefs, so they got the deluxe treatment in all the best local restaurants. Hank wasn't sure if this was enough to build a relationship on, but he couldn't quite pull away.

"I wondered if you might be able to knock off early," the doctor said. "Come eat with me. I need your advice."

"My advice?" That was a new one; usually Hank asked the doctor what to order, what to wear, what to read. Even so, he was annoyed by the doctor's evident belief that he could just walk off his job at a moment's notice. The produce manager at Whole Foods might not be as important as the coroner of Orleans Parish, but the fruits and vegetables couldn't very well arrange themselves. "Can't. I gotta be here until nine."

"Oh. Well, I suppose I'll go eat by myself then."

Hank allowed himself a small, private eye-roll. The doctor

wouldn't take himself anywhere nice; he'd drive out to the Piccadilly Cafeteria on Jefferson Highway and have a Spartan four-vegetable plate, poking sadly at his corn niblets while some poor fucker played the hits of the forties, fifties, sixties, and seventies on a Hammond organ. There would be a smattering of other lonely souls in booths around the room's bleak perimeter, and inevitably some old bat would be celebrating her ninetieth. The organist would segue from "What A Wonderful World" to "Happy Birthday," trolling for a tip. Altogether, it was about the most depressing thing Hank could think of.

"Hang on," he said as the doctor turned away. "Aren't you at least going to tell me what you wanted my advice on?"

"Sure," said Dr. Brite. "It was just a case. Semi-skeletal remains found under a house. Had a gourd where the heart should have been. I hoped you might be able to tell me what kind it was and whether it could have grown there. Never mind. I need a drink anyway."

Hank blinked. He wasn't that surprised by the idea of a gourd in someone's chest—two years of life in New Orleans had taught him that people would do anything to each other—but he was stunned that Dr. Brite would ask his opinion on a case, even one so obviously related to his work. The doctor considered himself a serious eater and dining expert, and had always made clear that he didn't believe Hank knew much about food at all. This caused Hank to compensate by acting as if he knew more than he did, and he usually ended up saying something stupid: he still cringed at the memory of the time he'd refused to believe there was real turtle meat in the famous turtle soup at Commander's Palace. He'd been certain it was just an expression, like toad in the hole or grasshopper pie. They didn't eat reptiles or amphibians in his native Hudson

Valley, and he still wasn't used to seeing alligator and frogs' legs on menus. ("Alligator is for the tourists," Dr. Brite had said contemptuously when he dared ask about it.)

The doctor wanted Hank's food advice *and* his forensic advice. The simultaneous ego strokes were too much to resist. "Claire can take over for me," he said. "I'll get my coat." Only after he'd turned and headed for the employee locker room did he remember that *I'll get my coat* was a largely meaningless phrase in New Orleans, even in October. He probably wouldn't need one for at least another month or so, and even then it would just be the Saints windbreaker Dr. Brite had given him.

They stood in the morgue's decomp room staring down at the dry brown thing on the autopsy table. There was a smell like leaf-mold and rotting potatoes, like sour earth and brine. Hank tried taking shallow breaths through his mouth, but the smell attached itself to his tongue, rich and sticky. The oyster po-boy he'd just eaten weighed heavily in his belly. He wished the doctor would give him some Vicks Vaporub to put under his nose like Jodie Foster in *Silence of the Lambs*, but he didn't want to ask. "I thought they didn't smell any more when they got dried out," he said.

"Oh, heavens no. They smell as long as there's a shred of flesh on them. They smell until you boil their bones, and Lord, do they ever stink while you're doing it."

The thing was folded in upon itself, faintly glossy, the color of yellowed shellac. It goggled up at him, horse teeth and fibrous black eyesockets, a crusted slit where the nose should be, a dry leaf in the place of its tongue … Hank made himself look away, not sure whether he was horrified or fascinated. It wasn't his first dead body, but it was the first that hadn't been sanitized, powdered, and nicely arranged in a viewing parlor.

"What happened to the hands?"

"We cut them off and soaked them. Trying to get fingerprints. That's about the only way to do it when the flesh is this dehydrated."

Christ, thought Hank, glancing back at the smoothly severed wristbones. *They just take you down to your components in this place. Parcel you out and send you on to the next department.* "What's this about a gourd?" he asked.

"I'm getting to that." Dr. Brite's gloved fingers spread an incision in the chest. The two halves of the rib cage came open like brittle wings. Inside, nestled among scraps of jerky that might once have been organs, Hank saw a ridged surface of yellow-orange streaked with dark green.

"This is *in situ*," said Dr. Brite. "He came in like this—and yes, he's a he, though I realize that's no longer obvious. Once I found it, I discontinued the autopsy until such time as it could be identified. Know what it is?"

"I'd need to see it closer"—Hank shuddered even as he leaned over the corpse, peering deep—"but it looks like a Crown of Thorns. Pretty little decorative gourd. *Cucurbita pepo*." He smiled a little, pleased with himself.

"What?"

"Its Latin name," Hank said modestly.

The doctor cocked an eyebrow and moved his microcassette recorder closer to Hank. "Could it have grown in there? Postmortem, I mean?"

"Well, it could grow in New Orleans, anyway. They're tropical plants—in the olden days, Crown of Thorns gourds were used as currency in Haiti." From the corner of his eye he saw the doctor wince. "What?"

"If there's one thing I don't want, it's a voodoo connection. Sore subject for me. Long story."

Hank wondered if the story had anything to do with the missing first joint of the doctor's left index finger. He had always wondered about that. All he said, though, was, "It doesn't have to be voodoo. Could just be a volunteer. Where was the body found?"

"Under a house in Mid-City. Raised camelback double. Vacant. Bad neighborhood. What's a volunteer?"

"A weed, basically. A plant nobody planted, but it grew anyway. See, the thing is, this gourd's a little bit unusual. If you buy a bag of decorative gourds at the supermarket, you'll get the Orange Warted, the Striped Pear, maybe even the Mini Red Turban, but probably not the Crown of Thorns. This might have come from a farmer's market or somebody's garden. Why don't you take a look at the stem? See whether it's broken or cut."

"I was getting to that." The doctor looked up. "You know, Hank, I may have underestimated you. I go to my friendly neighborhood grocery and buy a mango, and the checkout girl says *What's that?* No, excuse me, she says *What dat is?* I ask you a simple question about gourds and suddenly you're giving me their history and provenance."

"It's different at Whole Foods," Hank said, trying to sound modest. The truth was that few of his coworkers took as much interest in their departments as he did. Produce had always fascinated him—the varieties, the growing conditions, the politics of it—and he read up whenever he could.

The doctor grasped the gourd and gently teased it out of the incision. It was an odd-looking thing, ringed around its circumference by the series of pointy protrusions that were its namesake. Some of these were sharp; some were knobbed on the ends like bones. He examined it briefly, then put it in Hank's gloved hand.

"This stem was cut," said Hank. "See the sharp diagonal?"

"Meaning?"

"It didn't grow there. It was placed. And it's reasonably fresh."

"Again, meaning?"

"Whoever put it there didn't do it when the body was newly dead," Hank told him. "They came back and did it later."

Across the long causeway bridge that connected New Orleans to points north of Lake Pontchartrain, it was a different, colder world. Well, not really, but at least Hank could see a hint of autumn color, could smell a whiff of cider and woodsmoke. Or so he imagined; he was sick of New Orleans' relentless greenness, of the soft clammy air that sucked at his face and brushed the back of his neck like an unwanted lover's touch. It just wasn't right for the mercury to be above eighty in October. He didn't think he would ever get used to it.

The North Shore was only thirty miles away, but it felt marginally less tropical than the city. It had pine trees and those barely perceptible rises that Louisianians called "hills." The ditches were frosted with goldenrod and a purple flower Hank couldn't name. Roadside farm stands boasted pirate's booties of great orange-gold pumpkins, dried corn like pearls and rubies, mellowly gleaming jars of sweet potato butter. Of course the doctor wanted to stop at all of these, but Hank kept talking him out of it. "There'll be plenty of all that where we're going. I'm sure Gavin will be happy to get your business."

"Who is this guy again?" said Dr. Brite, though Hank had already explained twice. The doctor wasn't a very good listener sometimes. Well, most of the time.

"He's a farmer. We only get things like fresh herbs from him—most of our produce comes from California—but he sells to lots of the local restaurants, farm stands, the smaller supermarkets. I happen to know he grows gourds."

"And you think he can help us with the Crown Royal?"

"Crown of Thorns," Hank corrected. The doctor seemed to have liquor on the brain lately, and often on his breath too. Hank wondered if he should offer to drive, but the doctor didn't like to let anyone else behind the wheel of his ride, a 1988 Lincoln Town Car, burgundy with matching leather upholstery. It drove like a seagoing steamer and Dr. Brite treated it like a prize racehorse.

Since Gavin couldn't see them until after five, they had decided to make a day of it. They had lunch at the little brew pub in Abita Springs, which Dr. Brite declared one of the great underrated restaurants of the area for its hot wings alone. "The only ones that compared were the Apostle Bar's a couple years ago," he told Hank, stripping the flesh from one with his small, even white teeth. "They did a tequila barbecue sauce and a really nice blue cheese dressing, but the chef left to start an upscale restaurant, so of course he doesn't do them any more, and the ones at the bar are dreadful now."

The wings were good, very spicy and just a little sweet, a Platonic accompaniment to the smooth, nutty Fall Fest beer Hank and the doctor were drinking. Hank wasn't crazy about a lot of the food New Orleanians were so proud of, especially the fancy stuff, baked oysters in glop, fish mired in cream sauces and topped with mountains of lump crabmeat. He was grateful that the doctor enjoyed simple joints like this as well as the city's gaudier palaces of dining.

"I imagine you think hot wings were invented by Italians in Buffalo," the doctor continued.

"Well—"

"Perhaps. But Calvin Trillin suggests the dish was being cooked and sold by black people in Buffalo and elsewhere years, possibly decades, before the Italian bar made them 'famous.' Imagine that. White people co-opting black culture and taking credit for it."

Dr. Brite smirked. When they'd first met, Hank occasionally wondered if the doctor wasn't the tiniest bit racist, but he later decided it had just been his own Yankee PC-ness kicking in. "We're all red on the inside," the doctor was fond of pointing out when someone really *did* make a bigoted remark, "and besides, there's far less genetic difference between human races than between, say, a Great Dane and a Chihuahua."

If Hank was to be completely honest with himself, he had to admit that the corpse they'd viewed had reminded him a little of the doctor himself: dry, impassive, and apparently heartless. Yet there was a kind of heart there, just not the kind you expected. He would not have spoken these thoughts aloud for anything, no matter how persistently they kept running through his head.

With some time left to kill after lunch, they wandered over to a tree-shaded park near the restaurant. The doctor, a birdwatcher, had brought along his binoculars and went over to the creek to peer into the treetops; he said it was the fall migration. Hank only ever noticed birds in a vague way, colorful scraps of the landscape that didn't demand any further attention, so he sat on one of the swings and pushed himself back and forth. The semicircle of thick rubber pinched his adult ass, but not unpleasantly so. For the first time since he'd lived in New Orleans, he really felt that it was fall: a half-sad golden slant of light, the smell of the warm iron chain on his hand reminding him of school. He remembered the imaginary horse he'd had, Felicity—where had he come up with that faggy name?—flame-colored and azure-eyed, who coursed with him over endless grassy planes every time he rode the swingset.

The day was beginning to wane by the time they got to Gavin's farm near Folsom. Dry grass husked against the underside of the Lincoln as they pulled into the parking area. The golden slant of light had turned oranger and somehow meaner. Instead of a pleasant melancholy it gave Hank a sick lonely feeling somewhere deep inside, way down in a very young place where he didn't like to go much any more. The shadows beneath the vast gnarled oak tree in Gavin's front yard were velvety black, waiting to merge with the night.

"Someone actually *lives* here?" said Dr. Brite. "It looks like the stereotypical spook house."

It was a slightly ramshackle old Victorian with a mansard roof, but the last time Hank visited, the front door had been painted a cheerful violet and curtains hand-sewn by Gavin's wife had hung in the big windows. Now the house looked deserted, the porch rotting away, the windows like blind eyes. Through their unshrouded glass, Hank thought he could see long swaths of cobweb drooping from the ceiling.

"Gavin?" he called. "Elinor? You folks home?"

"What's that?" said the doctor.

Hank turned, afraid of what he might see. A tongue of wan flame had sprung from the roots of the oak and was snapping and wavering in the twilight. As the two men watched, another little flame joined it, then another. They did not burn warmly, but with a cool blue edge that made Hank think they were the earthly remnants of something dead.

"Will o' the wisp," Dr. Brite remarked almost casually. "They say if you can catch it, you'll have everything you ever dreamed of ..."

And then the doctor was following the flames, letting them lead him off into Gavin's fields, and Hank was following only because he didn't want to be left alone in this inexplicable place, this place where his friends were not and might never have been, this lost time between dusk and night.

"Doc," he called. "Doc, wait. Don't go with them. They're dead. They're all messed up."

The heel of his boot came down hard on something, cracking it open and partly crushing it into the black loam. Looking down, he could barely make out a broken Crown of Thorns gourd, the pulp leaking out as dark as blood in this terrible light.

"Hank?" said the doctor. "Hank, I could see the flames, but now I can't see anything. Come to me if you're there."

"Keep talking, Doc."

It wasn't *that* dark; they should be able to see each other. Hank groped through the veil of black-orange light, fainting-light, wondering what it would be like to exist here forever.

"Well ... er ... weren't those hot wings good? ... Calvin Trillin also said that like a good second-hand bookshop or a bad South American dictatorship, a superior fried-chicken restaurant is not easily passed down intact ... but of course some people don't think of hot wings as fried chicken ... and you *can* bake them in the oven, but I don't think they're ever as tasty that way, do you?"

A shameful urge flashed through Hank's mind, the urge to just turn and walk away, back to the car. The terrible light would let him go, he was certain. But Dr. Brite had the keys, and anyway he knew he could not leave the man here no matter how tiresome he got sometimes. Instead he kept groping toward the sound of the doctor's voice.

"Hank, I can hardly breathe." Dr. Brite didn't sound frightened, just very sad. Hank took another step, and his boot collided with something soft that squawked.

"Cognac, cognac. Cognac, cognac."

"What?" said the doctor. At that moment the black-orange veils of cloud parted and the good yellow light of the moon shone down upon them. Hank heard the doctor take a deep breath, almost a gasp. Strutting and pecking in the dirt around their feet were several large, fat birds whose black and white feathers reminded Hank of dotted Swiss fabric. The birds' bright blue heads were absurdly small, their bills red and sharp. "Cognac, cognac," said one, and another replied gravely, "Cognac."

They were a little like small decorative turkeys and a little like peacocks that had utterly failed to live up to their potential, but mostly they were like nothing Hank had ever seen before.

"These are guinea fowl!" said the doctor delightedly. "The French think they say *cognac, cognac.*"

"Yeah, I can hear that."

"Really? I think it sounds more like *buckwheat, buckwheat.*"

"Listen, Doc, maybe we should get out of this field."

"Oh, we're all right now. Guinea fowl are good luck. They bring sunshine and fecundity, and some say they can steer the living away from the land of the dead."

"You're shitting me."

"Not at all," the doctor assured him. "And they're also quite delicious."

Hank winced at this rather tactless remark, but before either of them could say anything else, they heard Gavin calling across the field: "Hank? Doctor? What in the world y'all doing out there?"

The farmhouse was in good repair when they returned to it, lit and welcoming. A jolly jack o'lantern perched on the porch railing, orange candle singeing its fragrant innards. Gavin's wife Elinor gave them hot cider spiked with cinnamon and cloves. There was a plate of fresh chocolate chip cookies on the table and a pumpkin-colored cat curled up in a chair.

"I don't know about guinea fowl steering you away from the land of the dead," Gavin said doubtfully. "They're real good for eating ticks and yellowjackets, though."

The doctor asked a few desultory questions about gourds, but it turned out that they weren't grown commercially in Louisiana; Gavin had only put in a few rows because he was fond of them. The doctor didn't appear upset that he had wasted his day off, and he didn't make any reference to the corpse he was supposedly investigating. He seemed vague, lost in thought. He had lectured Hank on various subjects all the way up here, but as soon as they got in the car to go home, he touched a button on the luxurious wood-grain dashboard and music blasted from the speakers: NWA's "Fuck Tha Police" at top volume.

"You know something?" said Hank. "You're a very strange man."

It was late when they got back to Dr. Brite's house. The doctor's five Oriental Shorthairs swarmed around their legs, vociferously irate at having been left alone all day. In the dark kitchen, the answering machine's red light appeared and vanished, appeared and vanished. The doctor reached for the button, hesitated, then pushed it.

"Doc? It's Linda Getty." Getty was a homicide detective who often worked closely with the coroner's office. She was tough and plain-spoken, and Hank liked her. "Listen, we finally managed to get some prints on that decomp that had the gourd in its chest—"

"I hate it when she talks about my patients that way," the doctor whispered. "Decomp. What an ugly word."

Hank had heard the doctor say *decomp* dozens of times, but he held his tongue.

"It shouldn't have took so long, but apparently Garrison thought Riccobono was soaking the hands, and Riccobono thought Garrison was soaking 'em, and guess what? The damn hands were just laying there in the cabinet, dry as ever.

"Anyway, we got the prints. Now this is weird, Doc, so listen close. They're real similar to yours. Not identical, of course, but they have more points of similarity than should be statistically possible. Garrison says he triple-checked and there's no mistake. I don't know what to make of it. Give me a holler in the AM, huh? Nighty-night."

The doctor held one of his hands up in front of his face, blinked at it, let it fall. In his eyes was that same lost, preoccupied look he'd had at Gavin's house. "Not identical, but similar," he said. "And the gourd was fresh. The heart was fresh. It wasn't dried out, not all the way. Not too late. Perhaps …"

"Perhaps what?" said Hank when the doctor fell silent.

"Just perhaps," said Dr. Brite savagely. "Just perhaps."

"OK." Hank held up his hands in protest. "Jeez."

"Sorry. I'm not angry—but sometimes I wonder if the world is angry with me. Life gets stranger and stranger, and science isn't teaching me anything any more. Stay with me tonight, Hank, won't you? I don't feel like sleeping alone."

Hank worked at the market until six o'clock on Halloween night, then drove over to the doctor's house, mindful of children darting across streets like blown leaves. Most of them weren't in costume, and Hank tried to tell himself it didn't matter; surely they could still feel the magic of the autumn night, the benevolent anarchy of extorting from strangers. Never mind that in his own childhood, planning and creating the costume each year had been at least half the fun. The kids of New Orleans had hard lives ahead of them, and maybe their parents didn't have money for costumes. If they wanted to make the holiday all about free candy, who was he to protest?

When he arrived at Dr. Brite's house, though, Halloween was in full force. Glowing skeletons and zombies heaved themselves out of the ground. Animatronic tombstones screamed and shook and laughed. A fog machine hidden in the bushes cranked out clouds of enveloping mist. Cars from all over the city pulled up to disgorge excited children. Some of the smaller ones had to be coaxed up the steps to receive a fat goodie bag from the doctor, who was dressed as a wicked witch. The effect of the distinguished-looking man in the seersucker suit, peaked black hat, and long spangled cape was odd even for New Orleans, and Hank heard one mother telling her little girl, "He ain't gonna do you nothing … or maybe *she* ain't."

"This seems a little out of character for you," said Hank, making himself comfortable on the porch swing with a handful of bite-sized Snickers bars.

"Nonsense—I do it every year. There's no such thing as 'out of character,' Hank. There's only realizing you don't know someone as well as you thought you did. Including yourself."

Hank thought about that as he munched his chocolate. He didn't understand what had happened with the body that had the gourd in place of its heart, and he didn't think the doctor would ever tell him. He only knew that since they had visited the North Shore and come home again, the doctor seemed renewed somehow. He was still a pompous, self-centered cuss who blathered about food when other people were trying to hold a serious conversation, but a certain sense of despair had left him.

Earlier today, Hank had found a Crown of Thorns gourd among a shipment of regular ones at the market. He'd put it aside to take home, and he planned to keep it in a place where he would see it often. Would it remain fresh? Would it dry and shrivel to a husk? He supposed he would find out.

If it stayed fresh, perhaps he and the doctor would take it away with them someday. Maybe they'd move to the country, buy a big old house with some land, grow their own vegetables. Raise a few guinea fowl, just in case of trouble.

Hank grinned at the thought, and the doctor smiled back.

Wound Man and Horned Melon Go to Hell

Dear Jesus,

I never thought I'd be writing a letter to You, but then I never thought one of my favorite restaurants would be in Kenner, either. You know how fashionable it is for New Orleanians to bash the suburbs: Chalmette is full of rednecks; Metairie is nothing but wall-to-wall strip malls; Algiers is where that dragon-lady city councilwoman and all the rich snots who think they're too good to live in the *real* city reside. You get the idea.

However, Kenner has always seemed a little different to me. I'm sure You know about the Procession of St. Rosalie, in which they parade a statue of a sweet little Sicilian girl through the streets because she saved their cattle from anthrax over a hundred years ago, when it was still a cowtown. Plenty of New Orleanians would say it still is a cowtown, albeit of a different sort. But where is our Procession of St. Rosalie? Where is our meatball cone, that peculiar yet compelling treat invented by Kenner's chief of police?

Where, for that matter, is our Bulgakov's?

Look. You know I'm the coroner of New Orleans; You see what I have to deal with. Hell—excuse me—sometimes I probably see it before You do. You wouldn't think I'd have a lot of time to spend reading Internet dining forums. But I do have a certain amount of downtime, and as You know, I love restaurants. I maybe love them a little too much, and take them a little too seriously, which is why I'm banned from that one board Humphrey Wildblood runs, but he has the palate of an old sneaker anyway. Whoever appointed him a food critic should be sentenced to a lifetime of Lean Cuisine. Whomever? Whoever. I think. Christ, I don't read enough these days, let alone write. Excuse me again.

Anyway, somebody calling himself "Bill C. Bubb" (but don't You believe it; nobody uses real names on these things; I myself go to unusual lengths of verisimilitude by posting as "Dr. B") posted that there was a new Russian restaurant in Kenner, and had anyone tried it? Of course I was intrigued, as I always am when any sort of new cuisine dares to poke a cautious head over the New Orleans dining ramparts. What did somebody once say about something or other? "The parts that are good are not authentic, and the parts that are authentic are not good"? That pretty well describes the state of ethnic food in the greater New Orleans area, except that most of it is neither. Well, we do have some pretty damn good Vietnamese—excuse me—oh, shit on it, You don't really care about these expletives, do you? I've never been able to believe You were that sensitive, not at this point anyway. I mean, God knows You've had time to grow a thick skin.

So I had to try out this restaurant. I am still separated from my husband, Seymour, though I hope to affect a reconciliation someday. These days I usually dine out with my … I suppose You'd have to call him a "boyfriend," though the word sounds perfectly stupid coming from anyone over 25. Hank. He manages the produce department at Whole Foods. Now, Seymour knew even more about food than I do. The worst thing about Hank isn't that he knows nothing about food; it's that he thinks he knows *all* about it because he can tell a jicama from a taro root. Granted, that's more than most people can do, but it doesn't exactly make him Brillat-Savarin. However, he is distractingly pretty, albeit in a grungy three-day-beard-shadow way, and he can fuck like a madman. Libido of a seventeen-year-old, but he actually knows what to do with it. Are You sure You want to hear this?

Bulgakov's, right. It's in the old El Patio building and still looks like an El Patio, with little wrought iron balconies and mariachi guys painted on the walls, which are a vivid blood red. The family is from the Ural and has been here four years. Apparently there isn't a great demand for Russian food in Kenner, at least not yet; an old couple was eating when we arrived, but they soon left and we were the only diners in the place. The waitress was an adorable innocent girl who rapturously described to us her favorite Russian dish, which, as far as I could tell, involved cottage cheese, sour cream, and corn meal. (It wasn't on the menu; apparently this was comfort food prepared at home.) When I ordered a vodka tonic she said, "Do you want that on the rocks or with ice?" I was so confused I said, "Straight up." So I had the world's only vodka tonic with no ice, and it was awful.

On the menu were Russian and Eastern European dishes along with strange-sounding versions of New Orleans standards such as Oysters Rockefeller. The Russian salad with red beans and sauerkraut was quite good, as was the borscht. My entree, Chicken Kiev, was a hard little football in a peculiar cheese sauce, but I'd only had it once before (while visiting a Romanov-obsessed colleague in Arlington, Texas, which is surely not the standard bearer) and Hank pronounced this version very authentic.

"You mean you read a Russian cookbook once?" I said.

He scowled. Prettily, of course. "Actually, no," he said. "I dated a Russian girl, if you really want to know. A Chechnyan refugee. She'd come to the U.S. as a mail-order bride. Said she left the guy because he drank even more than the Russian men she'd dated."

I sipped my iceless vodka tonic and wished I'd kept quiet. Do You ever get that feeling? I mean, just wishing You hadn't ratted Yourself out? Never mind.

Hank liked his entree, a mahi-mahi filet stuffed with walnuts and dried fruit in a pomegranate sauce. "I miss the good pome-granate molasses that used to come from Iraq," he said.

"What happened to it?"

"We bombed the factory."

I reached over and forked up a bite of his fish. It was way too sweet for me, but I didn't bother saying so, figuring he would take it as a criticism of his taste. Seymour never cared what I thought of his taste; he was secure in his likes and dislikes.

We tried to talk to the chef, but he only spoke Russian, and the only Russian phrases I know are "Yes," "No," "Pastry filled with sturgeon marrow," and "The soldier and sailor are gangsters." None of these was helpful, but we managed to convey our enjoyment anyway. I think. At any rate, everyone smiled and nodded a lot. It wasn't that the food was all that mind-blowingly good, but we had been amused by the experience and felt obliged to praise anyone who was trying to do something different amongst the moribund temples of fine dining in the greater New Orleans area. At least, I suppose Kenner is part of the greater New Orleans area. Sure it is.

Until just recently, the mayor and the police chief were brothers, and they attempted a sort of unsuccessful coup in the last election. All very New Orleans.

It wasn't until the bill came to the table that the real weirdness cropped up—and that, of course, is why I'm writing You.

I picked up the faux-leather folder (between a produce manager and a forensic pathologist, guess who grabs the restaurant bills more often) and opened it to check the total. Two hard little objects rattled onto the table. Mints, I thought; strange Russian ones. However, instead of candy encased in cellophane wrappers, they appeared to be tiny boxes. One was printed with a picture of Wound Man from the old medical textbooks, a pensive-looking fellow pierced with various swords, knives, arrows, and rapiers. The other showed what looked like an African cucumber, a odd-looking spiky orange fruit also known as a horned melon (and I didn't learn that from any Whole Foods manager, thank You very much). I handed that one to Hank and opened Wound Man.

The next thing I knew, I was in Hell.

I'm not sure whether I mean that literally. There was no fire, no ice, no pools of molten sulphur, no demons singing "Hukilau." The only thing I can compare it to is a very bad drug trip intensified a thousandfold, with no idea of why it began and no guarantee that it will ever end. I could feel that I was still seated at the restaurant table. If I tried a little, I could even still see the red walls and the mariachi guys and Hank beside me. But all that seemed ephemeral and unimportant next to the things that seized my soul and shook it. An endless parade of bodies on stainless steel tables, some of them my friends and loved ones, some heartbreakingly young, some brutalized in ways I could not bear to look upon but still had to catalogue in intimate detail. An aging face in the mirror.

A deserted stretch of interstate highway. A bed that was sometimes empty and sometimes filled with a stranger who shared none of my history, who did not know me well and did not interest me very much. A husband who had realized long ago that he was happier without me and would never return.

I dropped the tiny box, and the images faded, in a way. In another way, I suspected they never would.

I looked at Hank. He had opened his tiny box and was staring into it, horrified and rapt. I expected to see dead light spilling onto his face, but no such thing happened; whatever came out of these boxes went straight into the meat of the brain with no extraneous special effects. I reached over and gently removed the box from his unprotesting fingers. He blinked, then stared at me. Neither of us spoke.

After a while, the waitress reappeared at the table to collect my credit card. "Did you enjoy everything?" she asked.

"You might want to reconsider the mints," I managed to say.

A puzzled shadow crossed her face. "They are only chocolates from Kiev. We all love them, but no one else seems to. I urge and urge the owner to stop serving them, but he insists we must use up at least this batch."

I left her a biggish tip—it wasn't her fault—and took Hank back to my house and had feverish, unsatisfying sex with him. It was unsatisfying even though he had lost none of his skill or vigor, because I now knew that his were the wrong arms, his was the wrong mouth. I could hardly stand to have him sleep beside me, afterward, but I preferred it to sleeping alone. I guessed that was the new story of my life, or would be as long as I could find someone tolerable.

So now I write these words to You, Jesus. I suppose I am having one of those existential crises where people say things like Is

This All There Is and What Is The Point Of It All and Should I Just Blow My Brains Out. Except I'd do nothing so violent; I've seen the mess it makes, thousands of times I've seen it, and I know too many of the cops who'd have to clean it up. I am acquainted with arterial points that will bleed out in seconds without much pain; I have access to drugs that would simply send me into the long twilight.

Unless, of course, they didn't. I had never seriously entertained the possibility that there might be a real Hell, an actual place. I still don't believe it is a place one could find on a map, but now I wonder: would it be possible to exist in that state, that contemplating-your-own-eternal-darkness state, forever? And if so, would suicide send me there?

I am a problem solver by nature. I am incapable of silent, internal prayer. By writing this out, I am honestly asking You these questions.

Is there a Hell?

Did I see it?

Would You really send me there?

Am I insane for wanting to return to Bulgakov's? That borscht was honestly very good.

I didn't like the Chicken Kiev, though. Should I try the Beef Stroganoff next time?

Love,
Dr. Brite

The Devil of Delery Street

Mary Louise Stubbs was thirteen the year the family troubles began. She was called Melly because four of her younger siblings could not say her full name, or hadn't been able to when they were younger. Her fifth sibling, Gary, was only a baby and couldn't say much of anything yet. Once that strange and dreadful year was over, her mother, Mary Rose, would not allow its events to be referred to in any more specific way than "our family troubles." That was how Melly always remembered them.

Her memories seemed to date from the afternoon of her cousin Grace's funeral. Grace, the younger child of Mary Rose's sister Teresa, had been carried away by a quick and virulent form of childhood leukemia. Now everyone was busy pretending that she had been a saint among nine-year-old girls. With the terrible unambiguous eye of an adolescent, Melly saw only hypocrisy in this. Grace hadn't been any saint; she was actually kind of a sneaky kid who liked to pinch smaller children when no grownups were looking. Melly had loved her, but didn't see the need to pretend she was now perched on the knee of the Blessed Virgin Mary.

The Stubbs family was gathered in their regular pew at Sts.

Peter and Paul, a dusty old brick church in downtown New Orleans, and Melly was having a hard time staying awake. She didn't usually sleep during regular Mass, let alone funerals, but a scratching in the wall of her bedroom had kept her up last night. She'd meant to ask her father if he would buy some rat traps, but the memory of wakefulness had left her as soon as she brushed her teeth and combed her long, coarse dark hair. She had the Sicilian coloring of her mother, a former Bonano, as did most of the other kids; only Gary was shaping up to be Irish-fair like their father.

Now, though, she began to nod off. Her brother Little Elmer, the next oldest after Melly, extended a finger and poked her in the ribs. "Father Mike ain't *that* boring," he whispered.

"Shhh," she replied. Father Mike was young, with soft dog-eyes and a thick shock of wavy hair, and Melly had a little crush on him. Not a sexy crush, it would be almost a sin to think about a priest that way, but a little warm feeling in her chest whenever she saw him.

"You the one falling asleep, not me—"

"Y'all both hush," their father murmured from Melly's other side, barely audible, and they shut up. Elmer Stubbs was a mild-tempered man, but there'd be misery later if Mary Rose caught them talking during a funeral Mass. Fortunately she was at the far end of the pew, twisting a Kleenex in her small, expressive hands. It was warm for March, and occasionally she'd reach up to blot the sweat from her brow, though she always pretended she was patting her jet-black beehive hairdo. How Melly loathed that beehive! "It's 1974, Momma," she said frequently, "time to comb it out." And Mary Rose always replied, "Nuh-uh, babe, I don't want to look like a hippie," as if a slightly more modern hairdo would transform her from a diminutive Italian housewife into a pot-smoking flower child.

Melly sat up straighter in the pew, stretched her eyes open, and hoped the rat would depart for more attractive horizons by tonight. They lived in a poor neighborhood, the Lower Ninth Ward, but their house on Delery Street was clean. Melly knew it was, because she had to do a lot of the cleaning. Some of their neighbors' yards were full of chicken bones and crawfish shells and Melly didn't know what all else, scattered among rusty garbage cans and hulks of old cars. Surely a rat could fill his belly more easily at one of those houses.

Her wishes went unanswered for the time being; at home later, as she was changing the baby in the upstairs bedroom he shared with four-year-old Rosalie, she heard more scratching and a series of bangs behind the wall. "What you doing, Mr. Rat?" she muttered. "Building you a whole 'nother house back there?"

Gary laughed and showed her the clean pink palms of his hands, as he did when anybody spoke in his presence whether they were talking to him or not. He was the sweetest-natured baby she'd ever seen, and the only one of her siblings who made her think she might want kids of her own someday. He had a little fluff of sweet-smelling curly hair on the top of his head and his eyes were the warm brown of pecan shells, not so black you couldn't tell the irises from the pupils like her own. She pinned his clean diaper shut and hoisted him onto her shoulder. "You gonna kill that old rat for me?" she asked him, and he laughed again.

Life went on as usual in the big old clapboard house, Little Elmer and Carl playing touch football after school, Henry with the other seven-year-olds in the decrepit playground down the street, Melly watching after Rosalie and the baby while Mary Rose went to Mass or fixed dinner. The house smelled of garlic and red gravy, of boys, of the sweet olive bushes that bloomed on either side of the stoop in March. They were nothing to look at the rest of the year, but every spring they turned even the poorest corners of the city luxurious with their scent.

The rat was gone for a week or two, and Melly figured her father must have put down some traps. Then suddenly it was there again, scratching behind the wall above her bed. This time the sound came deep in the night and didn't seem funny at all. She had shared her bedroom with Little Elmer until last year, when her mother said a growing girl needed her privacy and made Little Elmer bunk with the younger boys. And Melly had certainly been a growing girl: she'd gained five inches last year. She didn't like sleeping alone, though, had never done it in her life and wasn't used to the way shadows could mass around you when no one was breathing in the next bed. The creaky old house was no longer the well-known friend of her childhood, but a strange place that wanted to trap her somehow. What would happen when it caught her? Melly didn't know, but something deep in her gut seemed to liquefy when she thought of it.

She lay awake listening to the rat in the wall. Little Elmer had moved his toys into the boys' room, and Melly had put hers away in the attic, certain she would never need them again. Even Trina, the baby doll who'd been with her almost since her own babyhood, was stifling up there in a heavy garbage bag to keep out the dust. The room felt very empty. If a shadow should appear on the wall, she would know nothing was there to cast it.

The rat gnawed more loudly. Melly sat up, meaning to bang on the wall and scare it away. She did so one, two, three times. The rat banged back in perfect imitation.

She drew away, indrawn air hissing between her teeth. No rat could have made that sound, three sharp, deliberate knocks. She extended her fist toward the wall, hesitated, then knocked once more. A mocking flurry of raps answered her, coming from the spot her knuckles had touched, then six feet above that, all the way to the right corner, to the left corner, to the ceiling, and finally under the bed. The mattress quaked. She flung herself off it, crossed the room without seeming to touch the floor, and shot into the hall screaming.

The next day was Saturday, and Mary Rose had to go to Canal Street to start looking at suits for Henry's First Communion. Carl tagged along in hopes of getting something from the bakery at D.H. Holmes. In a display of sudden, perceptive kindness typical to Stubbs males, Little Elmer volunteered to watch Rosalie and Gary. "Why don't you go shopping with Momma?" he said to Melly. "I bet she lets you get a dress or something."

"She's not gonna let me get any dress. I got all my spring school clothes already, and you know the house note's due next week."

"Well, but you like to look at stuff. Go on—I'll watch the babies."

"I ain't no baby," protested Rosalie, who was listening.

"I'll believe that when you get big enough to quit saying *ain't*." Little Elmer lifted her onto his lap. "Go on, Mel."

Full well knowing that her brother had given up a Saturday afternoon of street football in order to let her have a few hours away from the house that had frightened her so badly last night, Melly tried to enjoy herself. The life of Canal Street whirled around them, car horns, billboards, pink and gold neon signs, old ladies in their best shopping clothes, hippies in tattered regalia, a trio of lithe young black men with Afro picks embedded in their fantastic poufs of hair. Every breath was a mélange of exhaust, fried seafood, perfume, and, on the French Quarter side of the street, some mysterious tang that Melly thought might be the smell of burning marijuana. She walked beside her mother and admired the displays in the windows of the big department stores. She didn't argue when Mary Rose *tsk*ed at how short the skirts had gotten. The boys danced behind her making devil horns with their fingers and singing: "*Takin care of business … it's a crime … takin care of business and workin overtime!*"

"They don't say *It's a crime*," said Melly, who spent just as much time listening to the radio as they did.

"Yeah?" said Carl truculently. "What they say, then?"

"*It's all mind*, I think."

"That don't make no sense!"

"*Doesn't* make *any* sense," said Mary Rose.

"But Momma, *you* say 'don't make no sense.'"

It was an old family game, and all three children chorused with their mother: "Do as I say, not as I do."

As they were riding up the escalator at Maison Blanche, Melly felt safe enough to say, "Momma, what happened in my bedroom last night?"

"A bad dream," said Mary Rose firmly and without hesitation, as if she had been waiting for this question. "You just had a bad dream."

"I wasn't asleep yet, Momma. I was wide awake, and that's not any rat in my wall."

"You make an Act of Contrition tomorrow, babe. That rat ain't gonna bother you no more."

"An Act of Contrition?" Melly didn't know what she had expected her mother to say, but it wasn't that. "Why I gotta make an Act of Contrition? What'd I do wrong?"

"Nothing, Melly, nothing." They reached the top of the escalator.

Mary Rose stumbled as she stepped off it, and Melly reached to steady her. "It's just to be safe."

Melly saw that her mother's eyes were frightened.

"Just to be safe," Mary Rose repeated. "It never hurts to be safe."

St. Joseph's Day fell on a Tuesday that year, and Melly was allowed to miss school to join her mother on her altar-visiting rounds. They went to the altar at St. Alphonsus and the one at Our Lady of Lourdes, then a tiny one belonging to a lady in their own neighborhood, and last to the altar of Mary Rose's sister Teresa. It was generally known in the Stubbs and Bonano families that Teresa was rich; her husband Pete was whispered to make more than $10,000 a year. They lived across the parish line in Chalmette, in a one-story brick house smaller than the Stubbs' but far newer. No one had expected Teresa to make an altar so soon after the death of her child, but Teresa said St. Joseph had been helping her all these years and she wasn't going to turn her back on him now. "This year is more important than ever," she had told Mary Rose, and while Melly wasn't certain what she meant, Mary Rose seemed to take comfort in the words.

The altar was set up in the carport, three long tables groaning with roasted fish, stuffed artichokes, anise cookies, devotional candles, a big gold crucifix, and a tall statue of St. Joseph holding the baby Jesus. The statue was wreathed with Christmas lights that blinked on and off, creating an intermittent halo effect. Mary Rose tucked a few dollars into the brandy snifter that had been set on the altar for donations, took a lucky bean from a cut-glass bowl full of them, and grabbed herself a plate of food. "You want some spaghettis?" she asked Melly.

"No, Momma." Melly did, but she had vowed to go on a diet for Lent. She was already planning to make the Rosy Perfection Salad she'd found on a Weight Watcher's card, even though the picture looked like a bad car wreck garnished with parsley. Instead she joined some other kids, mostly cousins and neighbors, to hear the music in the side yard.

Teresa had bragged about having a live band, but it was just an accordion player and an old man with a microphone. As was often the case at any Italian party, they were playing "Che La Luna." The kids began a circle dance as the old man sang, "*Mama dear come over here and see who's looking in my window ... It's the baker boy and oh, he's got a cannoli in his hand ...* " The circle parted to let Melly in. On her right was her cousin Angelina. On her left was a boy she didn't know, maybe her age, with big brown eyes and a Beatle haircut. In fact, he looked a little like Paul. She hoped her hand wasn't sweaty as he grasped it. "*In the middle!*" cried the old man cried. The kids screamed with laughter as they raised their arms and crowded toward the middle of the circle. The music went faster and faster, and the dance followed suit. Caught up in the moment, she squeezed the boy's hand, and she was almost certain that he squeezed back. A strange warm feeling welled up just under her ribcage, like a line of electricity being drawn out of her.

She thought the shrieks of the women behind her were part of the festivities, so she didn't know anything was wrong until something hit her in the back. It didn't fall away, but clung there, heavy and hard between her shoulderblades. *A bug* was her first thought, but reaching behind herself, she could feel that it was bigger than even the largest New Orleans cockroach. Something cold, with four arms and a lumpy part in the middle. A crucifix—it felt like the big metal one that had been on the altar. Melly couldn't understand how it was stuck to her, and she couldn't pull it off.

"Get it off me!" she yelled. The band stopped playing with a squeal of accordion feedback. The other children backed away. The boy who looked like Paul wiped his hand on his pants as if cleansing himself of her touch. She knew the gesture was probably automatic, but that made it hurt all the worse.

"Please get it off me!"

Here came Mary Rose, pushing through the crowd of children, spinning her daughter around and yanking hard at the crucifix. It clung to Melly's back as if some immensely powerful magnet were buried deep inside her, perhaps where her heart should be. "Please, Momma," Melly sobbed, and Mary Rose yanked even harder, but the crucifix didn't budge.

Now here was Aunt Teresa with a little pitcher that had been sitting on the altar, a pitcher labeled HOLY WATER. She upended the pitcher over Melly's back. A couple of the kids giggled. "Pull on it again," said Teresa. Mary Rose did, and the image of Jesus came off in her hand, but the cross stayed stuck to Melly. Several women in the crowd crossed themselves and fumbled rosaries out of their pocketbooks.

Melly pushed away from her mother, out of the circle, out of the little fenced yard. She had never felt more alone and freakish than she did standing there in the sun-baked street, one small person with a big holy water stain running down her back and at least thirty people staring at her from the other side of a fence. The warm electric feeling abruptly left her and the cross clattered to the asphalt.

Everybody was silent except for one old lady still praying: "Hail Mary, fulla grace, the Lord is with thee … "

"Grace?" Teresa whispered. "Grace?"

Melly turned her back on all the staring eyes. There was a soft collective intake of breath. Through her thin nylon blouse, it was easy to see the raw red cross-shape that had been printed in her flesh.

Melly only had disjointed flashes of the next few hours. She remembered repeating through tears, "I'm sorry, Aunt Teresa, I'm sorry" as Teresa stood holding the figure of Jesus and the denuded cross, looking from one to the other as if she couldn't quite understand how they went together. She heard people telling each other what had happened: "Did you see the way it jumped off the altar, just *flew*?" She didn't remember the ride home at all; the next thing she knew, she was in her own bed, half asleep, rocked by some strange nausea that seemed to originate in her chest instead of her stomach. Over and over she nearly drifted off; over and over the bed jerked just as she slid over the edge of consciousness, yanking her back to wakefulness. "Please let me sleep," she moaned, and a voice answered her.

"*You can sleep when you're dead, Mary Louise …* "

It was a harsh and guttural voice, a voice that might have last spoken a thousand years ago or never. The words seemed to result from an intake of breath rather than an outflow, as if the speaker were suffocating. It was the worst voice Melly had ever heard, and yet suddenly she wasn't scared so much as angry. If this thing had a voice, then it had a personality, and if it had a personality, then she could damn well tell it why it shouldn't be pounding on her walls and making holy objects stick to her back. "Who are you?" she said, sitting up.

"*The Devil.*"

"No you're not. The Devil wouldn't waste his time scaring some poor girl from Delery Street. Who are you really?"

Silence.

"Are you Grace?"

Still nothing. She felt that she had offended it. And now she was frightened again; how had she dared to speak to such a thing, surely not the Devil but maybe some low minion? Even if it was only a ghost—she laughed at herself a little, thinking "*only* a ghost"—she oughtn't to be talking to it.

Melly sighed, got her beads out of the nightstand drawer, and started saying the rosary. She got all the way to the second decade before the beads were snatched out of her hands and scattered across the room.

Mary Rose got Father Mike to come over and bless the house. He made clear that it wasn't an exorcism, that he wouldn't perform an exorcism if she asked, that furthermore he didn't believe the Stubbs house was haunted; he was only doing it to put her mind at rest and maybe calm Melly down a little. Melly thought that was ridiculous. Right now she was the calmest person in the house. She found that she no longer had the warm little crush on Father Mike.

One day when her parents thought she was upstairs, she overheard the tail-end of a conversation between them. Though she knew her father was an uncommonly good man, she would never quite forgive him for asking Mary Rose, "Don't you think there's some chance she's doing all this to get attention?"

"No, I don't think so," Mary Rose had replied. "This isn't the first time crazy things happened in my family. You know that little end table my momma used to keep by her sofa?"

"I can't say I do."

"You know, Elmer, that little black table with the Italian patterns. It was hand-painted by my great-grandmother in Sicily. Lord, how that woman hated cursing and arguing—at least that's what Momma told me. Well, she passed away long before my grammaw brought the table to America, but whenever anybody in the house would start cursing or hollering at each other, the table would rise up and beat them!"

"Mary Rose, nuh-uh."

"I swear on my mother's sweet name. It happened to me a couple times, when I was real little and pitching a fit. I remember seeing that thing fly through the air toward my head—Jesus Lord! But when it hit you, it never hurt. It'd just tap you real soft, like it was saying, *You better behave*."

"What happened to it, then?"

"The effect just wore off, I guess. Teresa's got the table now, and you know how bad her kids cut up sometimes, but that table ain't moved in thirty years. At least not that I know of."

"Well, maybe this thing with Melly will kinda taper off."

"I hope so," said Mary Rose with a long-suffering sigh. "It's hard on her, and it's hard on me too."

It was not at all hard on the younger kids. They loved it, and got to the point where they would egg it on. "Bet you can't lift me up in this chair!" Henry would say, pulling his feet up in expectation of a ride. The spirit never gave him one, but sometimes it would tilt the chair and dump him onto the floor, reducing Rosalie and Gary to helpless giggles.

"Draw something in my book!" Rosalie would demand, leaving her scratchpad open with a crayon on top and hiding her eyes. When she looked again, often as not there would be a page full of meaningless scribbles.

"The baby done 'em," Melly said one time, trying to vacuum around them.

"He did not! He was right here by me the whole time, weren't you, Gary?"

"Lady draw," said Gary.

"Huh, you mean you can see it?" said Henry. "Aw, Melly, I wish he could tell us what it looks like! A lady, huh?"

"Shut up!" Melly told them. "Don't talk to it, don't ask it to do things, just leave it alone! You don't know how it makes me feel."

"It's not *yours*," Henry said unkindly.

"*Yes it is!*" she screamed at him. The startled look in his eyes made her feel bad, but she couldn't stop. "It is too mine! Do whatever you want, but give me ... give me ... oh, I don't know what I'm saying!" She ran from the room, leaving Henry to get up and turn off the vacuum.

Little Elmer and Carl did not enjoy the spirit and stayed away from home a lot that year, immersing themselves in boy-business. All in all, though, Melly thought it was amazing what people could get used to. When she heard scratching and raps in her wall, she rolled over and tried to go back to sleep. Sometimes it stopped there; sometimes things began flying around, toilet paper and jigsaw puzzles and sausages strewn around the living room, every flowerpot in the house turned upside down. Sometimes an object would hit her, but she was never hurt or (after the St. Joseph's Day incident) even seriously humiliated. Once when she was sitting in the kitchen watching Mary Rose make a lasagna, there was a popping sound near the refrigerator and an egg rose into the air. Mary Rose hadn't had any eggs on the counter, so it must have come from inside the fridge. It floated lazily toward Melly, then hovered over her head. *Great*, she thought, *it's gonna smash in my hair.* Instead it tapped her lightly on the forehead, then fell and splattered gaudily against the faded old linoleum. Melly got up to fetch the dustpan, no more upset than she would have been if a dog had piddled on the floor. Once it was clear that no one was going to be hurt, the incredible had come to seem almost normal.

She wondered if this had anything to do with being Catholic, with accepting as unquestioned fact the existence of saints watching over you, helping and perhaps even hindering your enterprises; with taking for granted that the wafer in your mouth would change into flesh, the wine into blood; with praying to a ghost. She did not ponder this very deeply, because she was not a deep girl and she knew no other way to be but Catholic. When she said her prayers, she sometimes added some extra ones for the spirit in case it was a soul in purgatory.

It never spoke to her again after the night it said it was the Devil. Melly thought it might be embarrassed to have made such a claim, or possibly embarrassed to have provoked her angry response, like an overtired child who doesn't realize he's being obnoxious until he goes a step too far and his mother yells at him. She did not feel that the spirit had ever been angry with her; in retrospect, even making the crucifix stick to her back seemed little more than a desperate way of getting attention. Why it had wanted her attention so badly she didn't know, nor did she wish to ponder the question.

The nights of rapping and banging came further apart; there would be two in a week, then one, then none for two or three weeks. When they did come, the raps and flying objects seemed weaker somehow, as if the force behind them was winding down. No further scribbles appeared in Rosalie's drawing pad. Gary, though he was talking a blue streak now, said nothing more about a lady.

As Melly lay in bed one night, she felt something strange happening in her viscera. At first she thought she was bleeding, but there was no wetness, only a sensation of something warm draining from her. She put her hand on the concavity beneath her breasts, but it began to tingle unpleasantly and she took it away again. A few minutes later the sensation stopped. She felt wonderfully relaxed. It was as if she had been in pain for a long time, and had gotten so used to it that she no longer noticed the pain until it stopped.

After that night there were no more noises, no more strange happenings at all. For some time there was an undercurrent of tension in the house and among the family, as if they were bracing themselves for another assault. None came. "I miss the ghost," Henry said at the dinner table one night.

Mary Rose turned on him. "There was no ghost in this house, young man! Say anything like that again and I'll warm the seat of your pants for you!"

Henry's mouth fell open, affording everyone an unlovely view of half-chewed braciola. *Poor Henry*, Melly thought. *That was probably the most exciting year of his life, and Momma's never even gonna let him talk about it.*

She didn't want to talk about it either, though. Henry would have to sift through his memories alone.

Another year passed. Melly grew a couple more inches, but nothing like the rapid stretch she'd experienced just before the odd events began. Gradually she stopped fearing that she was going to be a circus freak, the Giant Lady. She'd probably gotten some extra height from Elmer, that was all. She joined the math club at school, went out on a few dates, got involved with Sts. Peter and Paul's youth group. All she wanted in the world was to be a normal teenage girl; she wanted that so badly that she thought she could taste acceptance, sweet on her tongue, when other kids treated her as just one of them. Kids who had no idea that a crucifix had once clung to her back like it was a magnet and she was iron, kids who never suspected that something possibly dead had once knocked on her bedroom wall.

When the scratching started up again, so soft and sly that at first it might have been her imagination, she thought for one black moment of just putting a bullet in her head. Elmer didn't like guns, but crime in the neighborhood had begun to spiral upward, and he had one on the high shelf of the bedroom closet. Melly knew where the bullets were kept. But she didn't want to die, and she wasn't going to let this stupid mindless thing tempt her into it. She rolled over and went back to sleep.

At breakfast the next morning, the saltshaker rose off the table and floated across the kitchen. Henry's face lit up, and he began to say something. As Mary Rose's eye fell upon him, he shut his mouth with a snap. Everyone else ignored it, even Gary, who at three was exquisitely sensitive to the feelings and wants of his family. He got along with everybody, and wouldn't dare mention the floating saltshaker once he'd observed that the others didn't want to see it. Melly could see that Henry still wanted to say something, but she added her own glare to Mary Rose's, and he wilted.

There were a few more raps, a few more scratches. Then the sounds stopped again, and for a few days there was a distinctly injured air to the house, as if some unseen presence felt rejected. Then there was nothing except the usual vibrant atmosphere of a house full of children.

Melly had skipped St. Joseph's Day last year, but this year Gary and Rosalie were going to be angels in Teresa's tupa-tupa, the ceremony in which the Holy Family entered the home and were fed from the altar. She couldn't bear to miss that, so she squared her shoulders, steeled her spine, and accompanied the family to Teresa's house.

Cousin Angelina was playing the Blessed Virgin Mary. As soon as they got there, Melly saw her standing near the altar, slightly pudgy in a white dress, a light blue headscarf, and her usual pink-framed glasses that made her eyes look a little like a white rabbit's. She stuck out her tongue at Melly. Melly held her nose and crossed her eyes. "Who's gonna be St. Joseph?" she whispered to Mary Rose.

"Well, Teresa wanted Pete to do it, but he said that'd be incestuous since he's Angelina's father. So they got some boy from the neighborhood. I don't know his name." As she spoke, Mary Rose herded her pair of angels up the driveway toward the carport. They were dressed in white gowns with posterboard wings and tinsel haloes. Flashbulbs started going off as if they were walking the red carpet at the Academy Awards. Gary looked a little scared. Rosalie looked smug, as if she'd always known she was destined for stardom.

Drawing closer to the altar, Melly caught sight of St. Joseph, a tall, slim boy wearing a rough brown robe and carrying a crooked staff. He turned, and she saw that it was the boy who had held her hand in the circle dance two years ago, the boy who looked a little like Paul McCartney. The boy who had seen her crying in the street with the shape of a crucifix embedded in her flesh.

Just as she was about to look away, he gave her a smile so sweet it made her stomach flutter. "How you doing?" he said. "I looked for you last year, but you weren't here."

"I … I wasn't feeling too good last year."

"Well, nice to see you. Maybe you'll dance with me later, huh?"

"Sure." Then, before she knew what was going to come out of her mouth, she said, "But I'm staying out of the circle dance!"

For a moment he looked almost shocked, and she was sorry she'd said it. Then something else dawned on his face, a mixture of surprise and admiration. He hadn't thought she would have the guts to bring it up, she guessed. From the corner of her eye she saw Angelina watching them jealously.

"Yeah," he said. "I'd do that if I were you. This year the whole altar might just rise up and bash you on the head."

"You never know."

He turned away and headed for the house. Behind her, Melly heard Mary Rose urging the angels, "Follow Mr. Joe. Y'all gonna eat soon."

"I'll take 'em," said Melly. She coaxed Gary and Rosalie into the house, dropped them off with the ladies who were coordinating the tupa-tupa, and went into the kitchen to see if she could help with the food.

Aunt Teresa was at the stove fussing over a huge pot of red gravy. She turned and saw Melly, and for a moment fear flickered in her eyes, or maybe just sorrow. Melly wondered if she should have come after all. Then Teresa smiled, held out her arms, and drew Melly to her.

Later, as she was standing with Paul (whose real name turned out to be Tony, but she couldn't get that first impression out of her head, wasn't even particularly anxious to do so) looking at the altar, she saw the gold crucifix that had stuck to her back. She could tell it was the same one because there was a big blob of dried glue showing between the figure of Jesus and the cross. A rosary made of painted fava beans was looped over it, and there were oranges arranged around its base. Melly reached out a hand, hesitated, then gently touched the crucifix.

"Goodbye," she said under her breath, and was relieved when nothing answered her.

The Last Good Day of My Life
A True Story

This morning I was looking at the tide charts in the Times-Picayune, *and I said to Chris, "What if you were on Mars, and somebody sent you a* Times-Picayune? *You'd just lose it seeing all these names—Shell Beach, Caminada Pass, Chandeleur Light, Lonesome Bayou. You'd see the word 'Pascagoula' and burst into tears."*

—Author's journal, August 17, 2005

I had been two weeks in Australia, first in Melbourne on business, then up to the North Queensland rainforest to see birds. I stayed at Cassowary House, a birders' lodge near the small Aboriginal town of Kuranda, breakfasting each morning on fresh tropical fruits and toast with Vegemite while birds of paradise landed on the deck table and tried to steal the butter, watching the resident family of Southern Cassowaries: vast flightless birds taller than me, with plumage like glistening black grass skirts, iridescent necks, bright blue heads, fierce faces, heavy spurred feet for disemboweling, and great bony crowns atop their heads. Other than the mostly somnolent alligators of the Louisiana swamps, I'd never been around a wild animal that could easily kill me if it wanted to. However, no cassowary has murdered a person in Australia since 1923, and they did not murder me.

On the day before my twenty-four-hour flight home, I came down to Cairns, a small coastal city most visitors use as a jumping-off point to snorkel the Great Barrier Reef. Since water and I do not mix quite that well, I decided to just walk around looking at things, picking up restaurant menus, and trying to add a few shorebirds to my list. This is generally my way of getting to know any new place, with the added bonuses of reading the local paper and visiting a grocery store if at all possible. (I used to think Chris and I were the world's only supermarket tourists, always on the lookout for grocery stores of other lands, but I've since learned that there are more. It's fascinating to examine the different produce, meats, and— especially on the other side of the world—name-brand products such as condiments, breakfast cereals, cookies, and snacks that you've never seen in your life, but which have imprinted themselves on millions of Australian consciousnesses. Well, it is if you're of a certain mindset, anyway.)

I had booked a room, sight unseen, for one night only at the Club Crocodile Hides Hotel. I didn't understand this name at all and it made me vaguely uneasy, but it was cheap and I only needed it from about noon until five A.M., when I had to leave for the airport. Hardier souls might not have taken a room at all, but I like to have someplace to retreat to and I thought I might need a nap. Besides, there never seems to be anywhere to leave your luggage these days; everyone just automatically assumes it will have a bomb in it. The hotel was a big slightly shabby Victorian-looking building in the middle of a block of them, with wraparound verandas, disturbing dark red carpet in the corridors, and bathrooms down the hall. It gave me that uniquely Australian feeling of warm, slightly off-kilter Englishness, as if somebody had taken a down-at-the-heels London hotel and plunked it on the edge of the southern Pacific Ocean … which I guess is more or less exactly what somebody had done.

As soon as I had checked in, I shot right back out again. Downtown Cairns was a flattish, sunny, comfortable-feeling place— I always like beach towns—where every shop seemed to be a travel agency, a high-speed Internet café, or a liquor and souvenir shop. A chalkboard reading MANGO DAIQUIRIS caught my eye and I marked its location for later, then headed toward the Esplanade to look for low-tide waders.

The beach wasn't a beach as I know them. The major beaches of my life border the Gulf of Mexico, and while they may be slightly stained with crude oil, they have wide stretches of sand and water you can swim in without undue fear of death. In Cairns, the beach was an expanse of mud and shallow gray-brown water that began about four feet beneath the boardwalk and receded into infinity. Every ten feet or so there appeared a strident sign with a silhouette of a large, toothy crocodile and multiple warnings not to enter the water lest you be eaten by same. These huge "salties," the world's largest living reptile, like to sunbathe on the mudflats and snack upon the errant dog or tourist. Melbourne and Sydney are vastly civilized places, but once you leave them behind, the world as we soft Americans know it begins to fray at the edges very quickly; the signs also warned of sharks and stingers, which I guessed must be jellyfish but were represented in the graphic by a giant squid devouring a little stick man.

As I walked along the Esplanade, I saw a dismaying fish of my own. It poked its froglike eyes out of a tidal pool, then hauled its entire slimy gray-brown body out onto the sand and sat resting there, breathing air, for a few minutes before flipping itself back into the water. Then I noticed that they were everywhere. It was the mudskipper, an amphibious fish that can walk on land for short distances. Pretty tame by Australian weird-wildlife standards, I guess, but unlike anything I'd ever seen before. Stopping to sketch it and write down the names of the birds I'd spied, I found that I'd left all my pens back at the hotel. I was in an area of large resort hotels with no stores around, so I went into one of the resorts to see if they had a gift shop. The concept of a gift shop seemed to puzzle the young male receptionist a bit, but when I said I just wanted to buy a pen, he gave me one to keep. Though I could be wrong, I can't imagine a fancy hotel receptionist in any other country just handing over a free pen to any old Joe who came in off the street wanting one. (It had blue ink, which I hate, but you know what they say about beggars.)

By the time I had made a technically poor but serviceable sketch of the mudskipper, it was mid-afternoon, time to head back into town. Retracing my steps along the boardwalk, I passed an Aboriginal woman whose several children were playing at the edge of the muddy sand. She hollered amiably at them in some otherworldly twin of English: "You dressa no wine! Hump the car! Hump the car!" Otherwise the Esplanade seemed to have cleared out. I saw a couple of other bird geeks with binoculars and a few more parent-child sets at a small playground, but no one else.

Just before I cut back into town, the Esplanade opened up into a wide empty plaza where a young busker with a guitar was performing Oasis' "Wonderwall." His voice was very sharp and clear despite the ocean breeze that had begun to pick up. The horizon was infinite, cloudless. I suddenly knew in that way you do sometimes

that for the rest of my life, every time I heard that song, that plain-
tive male voice singing "And maybe … you're gonna be the one
that saves me …", I would remember this moment and treasure it.
There was nothing at all significant about it except that it was one
of those inexplicable moments where everything was perfect. I
think you probably only get a half-dozen or so in a lifetime, and
that's if you're lucky; I remember one at a New Orleans amusement
park when I was very young, one when I sat alone in an Amsterdam
coffeeshop as dusk fell, and one with Chris at an expensive restaurant where the meal turned out to be a culinary disaster (which in
no way diminished the perfection of the moment). That's about it
so far in this life.

I toured a multinational food court, nibbled some fish and
chips that were as bad as every other batch I'd eaten in Australia
(did that recipe somehow fail to translate from the British, or do I
just not like barramundi?), picked up some restaurant advertising
cards to take home to Chris, and left most of my chips for Willie
Wagtail, an iconic little black and white flycatcher who was perus-
ing the detritus of the food court the way House Sparrows ferret
out their livings from U.S. sidewalks and parking lots everywhere.
I finished off the afternoon at a sidewalk café reading the *Cairns
Post* (vague memories of a local child molestation scandal) and
drinking a fresh mango daiquiri that took thirty minutes to arrive
at my table, but was almost worth the wait.

I had one remaining goal in Australia: to buy a copy of Graham
Pizzey and Frank Knight's *The Field Guide to the Birds of Australia*,
which a friend had lent me in Melbourne and which was far superior to the guide I'd ordered before the trip. Somehow or other I
discerned that there was a shopping center eight or ten blocks from
the hotel. Walking there took me into a different part of Cairns, a

more livable-looking area full of backpacker bars, ethnic restaurants, and tattoo shops. The streets were still wide, flat, and full of pacific light. There were lots of black people here, whether Aboriginal or other I could not tell. To my intense joy, the first store I saw upon arriving at the Cairns Shopping Centre was a Bi-Lo supermarket. I spent a pleasant thirty minutes or so roaming the shelves, pondering strange fruits and labels, emerging with a large jar of Vegemite, a bag of bite-sized Violet Crumble candy bars, and an Australian food magazine. The bookstore had the book I wanted as well as a guide to the fauna of Tropical North Queensland I'd read at Cassowary House and coveted. I trudged back heavily laden but satisfied, eyeing restaurant menus along the way, making vague plans for the evening, discarding them, and forming others without consulting anybody, which is one of the greatest privileges of the solo traveler.

Back at the hotel, I tried to take a nap. My room opened onto the upstairs veranda and I was thwarted by drinkers speaking in incomprehensible swashy-sounding languages two feet from my pillow through a very thin wall. Toward dusk, I heard a great inhuman chattering and ventured onto the veranda myself. The trees opposite were full of Rainbow Lorikeets, hundreds and hundreds of birds, a prismatic shifting jumble of color: blue heads, chartreuse bodies, yellow collars, bright red eyes, bills, and breasts.

Through my binoculars, I focused on a single pair turning to look at each other. One bird spoke, the other replied with a slight nod, and they shot off to a new tree in perfect synchronicity. An Englishman came up and asked me what they were, and I let him have a look through the binoculars, then allowed myself to brag a tiny bit about the cassowaries. Aside from other birders, almost everyone I met in Australia seemed to think I'd been very brave to venture among wild cassowaries. Though I never had to protect myself past the point of avoiding eye contact when the patriarch came up and peered at me, I enjoy being mistaken for a hardened adventurer and readily agreed that yes, they *could* be dangerous.

Just before full dark, I admitted to myself that I wasn't going to get any sleep and headed back down to the beach in hopes of adding one more *rara avis* to my *album vita*: the Nankeen Night Heron, which looked in Pizzey & Knight like a browner version of the Black-Crowned Night Herons I could see any day in the park a couple of miles from my own house, and which a hardcore local birder had assured me I could easily find on the Esplanade around this time. He had even given me a landmark, one of the palm trees near the playground.

Downtown Cairns is built on a grid plan. I was only three blocks from the beach. Nonetheless, particularly after dark, I can get lost anywhere including my own neighborhood. I took a wrong turn, or veer, and ended up among casinos and construction, in a bleak area where no one else was walking. The beach remained maddeningly visible, but I couldn't seem to creep up on it. The streets led me astray. By the time I made it to the Esplanade, I was footsore and annoyed with myself. Glenn Holmes' palm tree was devoid of all avian life. I walked up and down, back and forth, straining my eyes. An occasional light gleamed out on the water—night boating among the salties?—which was otherwise black as a poacher's heart. Eventually I became unnerved by the infinity of the Pacific. I realized there was nothing out there until the Solomon Islands or maybe a stray Trobriand. Nothing separating me from it either, as in California where rocky cliffs often make the coast inaccessible. Nothing but a manmade boardwalk and some birdy, possibly crocodile-infested mudflats between me and that vast watery galaxy.

I don't mind feeling insignificant; in fact I usually feel insignificant, but vastness is just plain scary. Though the Pacific is nothing compared to the vast eternity of death, it's eternal enough to kill a man, which should be sufficient to unsettle any nervous constitution. I decided a vague bird shape out on the flats was a Nankeen Night Heron—there is really nothing else it could have been—and cut across the grassy verge between the boardwalk and the main beach road, back toward the vulgar, mortal, comforting lights and crowds.

The food court of earlier in the day had been magically transformed into the entrance to Cairns' Night Markets, a maze of stalls selling every kind of Australian-themed tourist tat imaginable: stuffed plush kangaroos, pearls, crocodile skins, deadly spiders encased in Lucite, potholders with kookaburras painted on them, T-shirts by the thousand. When I stopped to examine a pair of men's cargo pants made from some wonderfully soft and durable fabric, the handsome (if slightly leathery) guy manning the stall tipped his bush hat, said, "'Ow yer goin', gel?" and helped me look for my size, which he ended up not having. Those pants were the only thing I would have bought in all the Night Markets, but it was fun wandering through them.

The final adventure left to me was dinner. I had seen two kinds of restaurants in Cairns, little ethnic places much like you'd find in any other city and appalling-looking temples of anti-cuisine obviously aimed at tourists; one advertising card for a joint offering "Real Australian Cuisine" restaurant showed a plate whose edge was bammed with the words "G'Day Mate" in loopy letters formed from some kind of red sauce. (*Bam*, verb: In kitchen lingo—New Orleans kitchen lingo at any rate—to apply silly decoration to the edge of a plate: words written in chocolate, designs in paprika, etc. Poss. deriv.

Emeril Lagasse.) The lone exception was an interesting-looking place I'd passed on the way to the shopping center. The Red Ochre Grill offered modern Australian cuisine, but in a seemingly intelligent way, without any cutesy slogans or obvious bammage; their menu featured "Australian seafood, Australian game meat, bush food and regional Australian cuisine." My meal was seasoned with all sorts of interesting fruits, leaves, herbs, and barks found in the bush, the rainforest, and other antipodean habitats. I had lovely cold metallic lacy-edged Tasmanian oysters, an "Australian Antipasto Plate" (smoked wild-spice-crusted kangaroo with horseradish cream; crocodile wonton with capsicum jam; emu pate with bush tomato-chili sauce; smoked swordfish with pickled ginger and wasabi; and a peculiar little thin-omelette/roast-capsicum roll), a wonderful ineffably salty-and-spicy lemon myrtle sorbet palate cleanser that tasted the way the rainforest had smelled, and a selection of Australian cheeses. Kangaroo has been delicious every time I've tried it. Crocodile isn't up to much in my opinion, unsurprising as I don't care for its Louisiana cousin either. The emu pate was rich and livery; I wondered whatever happened to all those emus farmed by American entrepreneurs in the early '90s. The cheeses were a King Island Blue (mushroomy, complex), a "rich cheddar" (sweetly sharp), and an alleged Camembert (far too young, 'twas child abuse to serve it). When he heard I liked the blue, Chef Craig Squire sent out a Costello Danish blue for me to compare. One sign of a good chef is that he appreciates cheese enthusiasts. The Red Ochre Grill took wonderful care of me—the hostess even made me a photocopy of the menu without being asked—and I forgive them for having the worst dessert name ever: "Chocolate Slut."

There is seldom any pleasure in admitting to strangers that you are a writer. Paul Theroux claims that it shuts people up just when you want to hear them talk, but in my experience it brings on an embarrassing barrage: "What do you write? Anything I've heard of? Where do you get your ideas? You know, I've always wanted to write a book ..." Even so, I was in such a good mood after the meal that when the nice French/Australian couple at the next table started talking to me (they wondered why I was making notes), I didn't even claim to be a mortician or an ornithologist specializing in spoonbills; I admitted to my profession and gave them a business card with the names of my last two books written on the back. Then I staggered back to the hotel in one of the most elusive pursuits I've ever attempted: catching a few hours' sleep in a hotel room above a pub in an Australian party town on a Saturday night.

> *Upon occasion I have had the pleasure to regale ya*
> *About the avifauna of the continent Australia.*
> *You may think you know it well, but p'raps you*
>   *haven't heard:*
> *In all this wondrous land there's not a single hummingbird.*
> *You might think they'd have come across on ships from*
>   *other nations,*
> *But maybe not enough to start their breeding populations.*
> *The Aussies feel the lack of iridescent flying jewels,*
> *But in this, as in other things, they surely are no fools;*
> *With 100,000 honeyeaters they've filled this eco-niche,*
> *And so for want of hummingbirds they hardly ever bitch.*
> *Besides, to long for any bird is really quite hilarious*
> *When you've the chance to view the* Casuarius casuarius.

—Doggerel composed on my flight home, July 24, 2005

I saw 142 species of birds on that trip, 136 of which were lifers (species I'd never seen before). I wouldn't see another lifer until the tenth of January, 2006, when an American Goldfinch landed at the feeder outside the window of the New Orleans apartment we'd escaped to after the post-Katrina failure of the federal levee system destroyed our home and tore our lives apart. When I think back on the trip, my mind automatically marvels, "And we only had a month to live!" This seems nearly blasphemous given all the people who really *didn't* live, but I can't help myself; the world as I knew it ended on August 29, 2005.

I often think that day spent knocking around Cairns was the last good day of my life. I wasn't unhappy to return from Australia to New Orleans, but as soon as I got home, I had to rush to finish a novel for an editor who would ultimately seek to exploit my Katrina experiences and cause another, smaller apocalypse in my life. I finished the first draft of the novel and e-mailed it to my agent the night before the storm hit, convinced I was going to die. We did not stay, did not die, and that haunts me as much as anything; even so, the only adventures ahead of me were nightmare ones I'd never have chosen.

> *We spend our days waiting in gas lines, picking up ice from FEMA and Red Cross sites, crying, and reading. At night we read by flashlight or candlelight. I reread* Misery, *finished it in yesterday's gas line, and read half of it again before I got up to the pumps.*

> —Author's journal, September 4, 2005

That was the next time I consciously realized that I was having an adventure. I haven't been as fond of adventures since then. Nor have I left Louisiana very often. After Katrina, there were people trapped away from New Orleans who didn't know if their loved ones were alive for days or weeks. I sometimes think about how, if I had gone to Australia a month later, this could have happened to me.

After Katrina, there were plenty of people who couldn't bear to return to New Orleans. I may well be the only person who, having returned, can't bear to leave again.

We say we cannot face things and then we go on facing them. Even so, I am not at all sure I could have faced the events of 2005 and 2006 without that trip to look back on: all the birds, the heart-piercingly beautiful places, the fascinating food, the kind people. This is why someday I will force myself to travel again. Ignatius J. Reilly reminds us that outside the city limits of New Orleans, the heart of darkness begins. I miss the heart of darkness. Since I returned from exile a couple of months after the storm, New Orleans and I have lived in each other's pockets, gotten on one another's nerves. While I will always live here, I need to relearn how to leave every now and then.

> *… I've canceled my trip to a conference in Bremen, Germany, this summer. I had looked forward to my first trip to Germany and was hoping to visit Amsterdam afterward—it's one of my favorite cities in the world, and I've not been there for six years now—but Chris wasn't going to be able to go with me, and every time I tried to make myself sit down and buy my ticket, I felt the beginnings of a panic attack. I hope someday I'll again be able to leave New Orleans during hurricane season, but this year is too soon, especially to go all the way to Europe or somewhere else from which I couldn't fly home in a couple of hours … This is unprofessional and unlike me, but*

*the events of the past eight months are utterly without precedent in
my life and I don't dare ignore my gut feeling about this. I should
never have agreed to the trip in the first place, but I guess I thought
I'd be healthier by now, not a bigger mess than ever.*

—Author's journal, April 13, 2006

Until I overcome this, there will be no more truly good days
no matter where I am. No more cassowaries or mudskippers. No
more "Wonderwall" on the Esplanade. No more adventures except
maybe the kind you're forced into. No more coming home.

During one of our interminable conversations in which we at-
tempt to process what has become of the old life that still haunts us,
Chris pointed out that one of the great comforts of home is being
able to take it for granted. No one in the areas affected by Hurricanes Katrina and Rita can take "home" for granted anymore. In
the deepest recesses of our hearts, I doubt any of us ever will. We are
a damaged people, more accustomed to celebrating than mourning,
impatient with our own self-pity, trying to figure out what happens
next. A woman interviewed in a short movie about St. Bernard
Parish (a 1794-square-mile area where virtually every structure was
severely damaged or destroyed) told the filmmaker, "I got crying
days and I got no days." This sums up the day-to-day experience of
life after Katrina better than anything else I've heard.

Yet people are coming back to St. Bernard, and to New Orleans
with a vengeance. The debates you hear about "whether New
Orleans should be rebuilt" are moot: it's already happening, and
while we hope for the money to make us whole from the govern-
ment whose incompetence destroyed us, we'll do it with or without
that money. Nobody else gets a vote. I can't deny that life in New

Orleans is rough right now ... but to mash up William Butler Yeats with one of our beloved native sons, clarinetist Pete Fountain, "Some rough beast, its hour come round half-fast, slouches toward Bethlehem to be born."

Appendix:
Alternate Order of Stories

As detailed in the foreword, I've provided this appendix for folks who would prefer to read the Stubbs family short stories according to the chronological order in which they occurred in the characters' lives. Titles in parentheses are from my 2003 collection *The Devil You Know*, available from Subterranean Press in a signed/limited hardcover edition and from Gauntlet Press in trade paperback. For truly anal types, I should mention that the order of the stories from *The Devil You Know* is debatable; all three stories were written within a year or so of each other and all are intended to take place around the same time. Someday I'll get around to making a Liquor/Stubbs family concordance and will be able to pinpoint these things in a far more exact fashion than any sane reader could possibly desire.

"The Gulf," very much a *post*diluvian tale, does not appear in either book. It will see its first publication in a forthcoming Subterranean Press anthology and will be reprinted in my next collection. I include it in this appendix for the sake of future

completeness (though, since I intend to keep writing Stubbs family
stories, no such appendix is likely to remain complete for long).

"The Devil of Delery Street"

"Henry Goes Shopping"

"Four Flies and a Swatter"

"The Working Slob's Prayer: Being A Night in the History
of the Peychaud Grill"

"The Feast of St. Rosalie"

("Bayou de la Mère")

("A Season in Heck")

("The Heart of New Orleans")

"The Gulf"